A Pawn for

Malice

By

Cynthia Roberts

D1737984

Praise for Her Novels

"If you are looking for an enthralling story with plenty of heat, humor, and adventure, look no further!"

~ Romance Junkies

"Roberts' writing is solid, flows well, her angle is thought-provoking and descriptive details keep the pages turning. Roberts' literary contributions may be worth following."

~ IndieReader

"This was a very sweet novel. There is no other way to describe it. Unchained Melody is a clean, passionate, and very good romance that you will love to read again and again. Pamela's journey is honest, something that every working woman can relate to. She is a great character, and Gavin is a very cool guy. This is perhaps the first romance novel I have read this year that is smooth, well-conceived, and very well written."

~ Readers' Favorite

Chapter One

The swollen corner pockets of the striped, vinyl canopy overhead was near to bursting despite the protection it provided from the torrential downpour. Mindlessly, Jessica stared at the quarter-sized holes the pelting rain was carving into the ground surrounding her and the other members of her dead husband's family. She noticed how those in attendance were failing miserably at maintaining control of their umbrellas, as the forceful winds wrestled to pull them from their grasps.

Streaks of lightning illuminated the sky above distracting her attention. Her petite frame shivered, as she looked up at the menacing sky. The chilly autumn winds penetrated her thin raincoat and whipped at the veil covering her heart-shaped face. The dark mahogany casket in front of her was beautifully draped with a blanket of white gardenias and yellow roses. Despite that her husband's lifeless body occupied its confines, she felt void of all emotion.

She wanted nothing more than to see this day come to an end. Her husband's parents, Hal and Lorraine Wilton, were playing their grieving role for the media and those in attendance impressively. It sickened her to have to stand there beside them.

What a charade, she thought, as she gazed to her right at Father Mulcahy, pastor of St. Augustine's church.

He was doing his very best to offer some semblance of closure. Jessica knew Father Mulcahy viewed her in-laws 'pretend show of grief' a complete sham as well. If it wasn't for her pastor's support and refuge at times, Jessica knew she would be the one lying there in the casket instead of Richard.

Her eyes slowly scanned the faces of the mourners standing before her. Most were merchants from town, who she knew were there more out of fear, than respect for the Wilton name. The entire front row of onlookers shuffled forward closer to the casket, as Father Mulcahy cleared his throat to conduct the final prayer.

Another gust of wind caught the pastor's wide-sleeved surplice and puffed him up like a balloon and threatened to lift him skyward. Jessica could not help but smile, as she watched him wrestle to maintain some sense of reserve and control. He was such a witty man, who could stir someone to laughter faster than the winds that lashed about him. His soft Irish brogue could calm the most unsettling soul like a mother's lullaby.

Jessica sucked in a deep breath and let it out slowly, as he raised his arms heavenward and began the blessing.

"Dearly beloved. We gath'r here befar ya t'day to bid farewell to Richard Michael Wilton, a lad loved and …"

Jessica rolled her eyes in disgust. It was going to take every ounce of strength she could muster to get through this ceremony.

Dear God, she silently prayed, *give me strength … pa …leez.*

Absently, she reached beneath the dark veil she wore, and rubbed her bruised and swollen cheekbone. It was throbbing like a bad toothache.

Would she ever forget, she wondered, as the ache began to remind her of that terrible evening?

Her husband's rage was the worse it had ever been the night he died, driven by the alcohol he had consumed and his heinous reaction toward her evening out in the company of her Aunt without him. She had been raised to be a strong, compassionate, and independent woman. The apple did not fall far from the tree, where he was concerned though. Like his father, Richard was dominating, controlling, abusive, and a womanizer.

Their one-year marriage was a mockery of what true love was supposed to be. Richard did not prove the man he had projected during their courtship. He had only pursued her, because his father had ordained it. She was, after all, heir to the Newcombe Dynasty. It wasn't long, before abuse became a part of her everyday existence.

Their argument that night, had turned terribly heated, when she announced her plans to divorce him. He had caught her off guard with a sucker-punch that had sent her reeling backward. He wasted no time climbing atop her, his hands circling her throat, squeezing until she was on the edge of greeting death.

She remembered the sneer upon his face, as he slowly reduced the pressure around her throat and then rolled off her. He had watched her crawl on her hands and knees to escape him, her eyes blinded by stinging tears, as she tried desperately to suck air back into her lungs.

When he had attempted to rise, he weaved, then stumbled, losing his balance, and falling onto their glass coffee table. As it imploded, it afforded her the opportunity to seek refuge in their bedroom. She had managed to lock him out, as she retrieved the small snub-nosed revolver, she knew Richard kept in his Gentleman's Chest.

She had dialed 911 and told the dispatcher Richard attempted to choke her and she feared for her life. The dispatcher knew she was in possession of her husband's gun and promised to stay on the line with her, until a police unit arrived. The dispatcher heard Richard's threats to kill her, when he broke the door down. They had recorded her terrifying pleas for them to hurry and her blood-curdling screams, when the door's panel splintered apart and the shot that went off, killing her husband instantly.

Jessica shuddered, as tears streamed from her eyes. It was over. The District Attorney exonerated her based-on self-defense. Now, all she had to do was get away from Hal Wilton, who she knew, would do everything in his power to stop her. She gazed upon the casket still feeling hopeful. Nothing was going to stop her. Not even the great Hal Wilton.

The party she had attended with her Aunt the night that Richard had died, had been a liberating and glorious reprieve for the short while they were together. What she hadn't expected, was her immediate fondness for the handsome Senator from upstate New York the party had been hosted for. However, brief their introduction was, he was a man that was hard to forget.

Sen. Gallagher was the kind of man a woman wanted to see his slippers under her bed, and his body in it. Despite his charm and formidable, good looks, he stood behind a political platform she respected. Jessica understood why her Aunt supported his re-election for office so adamantly. He was a decorated Special Forces Marine veteran and a well-respected former police detective for the City of Albany. Her Aunt had confided that evening, that when she told the Senator of Jessica's degree in public relations and communications, he was interested in speaking with her about a vacancy in his executive office for Director of Communications.

Jessica never had the chance to have that talk, since he was whirled away on some state emergency. Just to know that chance was hers, gave Jessica the kind of hope for escape she could cling to. She knew that her Aunt would help her accomplish that goal.

I wish I was there right now, she admitted silently.

`There was nothing she needed more, than a new start, knee deep in a position that would fill her days and many evenings, working for a distinguished senator, who was bent on changing the world. If it wasn't for her Aunt Florence being called away for an emergency board meeting, Jessica knew her Aunt would have been there right now by her side, striking fear into the likes of Hal Wilton.

She watched as those before her shuffled uncomfortably, exchanging nervous glances amongst themselves. She pitied them for the mindless puppets they had become, and detested Hal for making them that way. She shot her father-in-law a look of disgust.

Hal Wilton reined with tyranny both over the town he owned and his family. Even now, they stood high upon a dais, separating them from the "little people", as he so often referred to the townspeople as.

Jessica jumped with a start and stiffened when Hal's left hand glided along her back and began to massage it seductively. As his palm slid to her derriere and cupped it possessively, she reached her left hand behind and dug her manicured nails into his flesh, until he released her. Even though he could not see her face, she still sent him a look of disdain.

"Stop it!" She hissed in a voice that was low yet menacing.

She took a quick step sideways and looked about to see if anyone witnessed the exchange. She wanted nothing more than to slap the snicker from his face, as he then reached his arm about his wife's shoulder, pretending to be the consoling husband and grieving father, spurring his wife to whimper even louder.

She shook her head slowly, despising the display. She didn't exactly hate the woman. She felt … what? Not respect … not love … maybe, empathy. She noticed the tears streaming down the woman's porcelain cheeks, still ageless and beautiful. It was so out of character for the woman to show any kind of emotion, as emotion caused wrinkles. Heck! The woman's lips were as tight as her newly-lifted ass.

Her mother in-law loved no one more than herself. She never once showed any signs of outward affection for her son. Jessica understood why. He was a clone of his father.

You failed miserably as a mother, Lorraine, she quietly chastised. *His death was partly your fault too, for not standing up to that bastard you married.*

Jessica scanned the faces again before her. The words spoken by Father Mulcahy did not penetrate her brain. Nothing he said mattered really. This probably could have all been avoided, if she had left Richard, when things had started to get bad. She was so naïve then, believing he would change, believing he would realize how wonderful she was and how much she had loved him.

Life had not been fair and dealt many a lousy hand. First, her mother died, giving her life. Her dad was killed in a plane crash when she was six. And then, her marriage to one of Maine's "Golden Boys," turned out to be a travesty.

She knew that her fate would have proved differently though if her Aunt had been the one to raise her. Instead, her paternal grandmother was given custody and when the time was ripe, she fell prey to Hal Wilton's charm and control. Unbeknownst to Jessica, they had connived a plan to bring his son and her together in marriage.

Jessica's marriage never had a chance from the on-start. Richard did a magnificent job disguising himself as an abuser, drunkard, and womanizer.

He had cast a spell over her with his magnetic charm and striking good looks! Every debutante in New England wanted to be Richard Wilton's girl. Instead of chasing after the stable of females at his fingertips, he had zoned in on her ... a petite, green-eyed innocent with long, wavy, brown hair. What a fool she had been to have played right into his hands! She was the total opposite of the bevy of blonde amazons with lustful eyes, who did everything to catch his affection.

Why didn't I realize ... see him for what he truly was back then? It was all just a lie... a terrible, deceiving, and hurtful set up.

The minute the ink dried on their marriage certificate; Richard's true persona reared its ugly head.

It won't happen again! She silently vowed. *I will NEVER be duped like that again!*

Jessica was snapped back to reality, when Father Mulcahy shook holy water out over the casket and a splash of it soaked through her veil and onto her right cheek. She shifted and forced herself to focus on the priest's final words, as he continued to sprinkle the length of Richard's mahogany casket.

"Father, we ask ya ta bless Richard's final resting place, as well as his soul, and ta watch ov'r his family, especially, his beautiful widow, Jessica. May the peace and glory of God's luv be with all of ye, now and forev'r, Amen."

The rain finally began to dissipate to a light mist, as the congregation began to disperse. Everyone except for Father Mulcahy departed without sharing a single word of sympathy. She watched the priest hesitate only briefly, before approaching her in-laws and finishing with his pastoral duties.

After extending his farewells to her in-laws, he turned and briskly closed the short distance between them.

Jessica's heart warmed, when he sent her a vibrant smile and opened his arms wide, as he drew near. A sob caught in her throat, when he tenderly embraced her and rocked her like a young babe.

"Ah, Lassie," he cooed. "I be fearin' you'll be tormented if'n you don't get away and soon." He patted her head tenderly.

She stepped back slightly and tilted her head, so she could look up into his soft hazel eyes. He was a gentle giant of a man with handsome features. She smiled when the wind tufted his thick pumpkin-colored locks into the air.

"Father," she sighed heavily, "I'm working on that. I'm vying for a position in Albany, but I'm afraid Hal will do everything to make my departure a difficult one."

"I may be straight off the boat, Lassie," the priest replied with a wave of his point finger, "but, we had our share of bullies like yer father-in-law too! You must promise ta call me, if'n ya need some help getting away."

Jessica looked about nervously.

The priest noted her reaction, pointed ahead and protectively drew his arm about her waist, and escorted her a few steps away from the dismissing attendees.

"Do ya have something in mind already? I'm serious now. If'n you need my help, you just say the word," he offered, patting her shoulder affectionately.

She smiled warmly and nodded.

"I do as a matter of fact." She turned slightly to look over her shoulder and make sure that Hal wasn't sneaking up behind them. "You know my Aunt Florence."

He nodded knowingly.

"Well," Jessica continued, "She just returned from a long business venture and I'm to move in with her, until I can find a place of my own."

Father Mulcahy's smile was one of content.

"Good. I suggest ya do that quickly. We both know Hal is an awful man." He stepped closely and reached out to tenderly place her face between his brawny palms. "If'n you need ta escape in the dark of night, call. Me life is a bor'n one and could use a lit'l spice now and then."

Jessica giggled.

"I just love you, Father Mulcahy, and going to miss you so much." She drew his hands from her face and held them in front of her. "Thank you. Thank you so much for all your support."

She rose up on her toes and hugged his neck tightly, whispering softly into his ear, "I'll never forget all that you have done for me. Never … ever."

He patted the back of her head and replied with a voice filled with emotion, "I will miss you, child."

"Me too," she squeezed him fiercely and stepped back. "I promise to call you, when I'm safe in Albany, but you mustn't breathe a word to anybody. Hal's got ears everywhere."

He kissed her forehead tenderly and tapped her nose with the tip of his finger.

"Yer secret is safe with me." He replied, as he turned and walked away.

Jessica watched his departure, until he was gone from sight. She was taken by surprise and squealed with fright as a vice-like grip encircled her upper arm and spun her about forcibly, making her fall hard against her father in-law's chest.

His pearly whites gleaned, as he glared down at her.

"Wasn't that a touching scene?" He snarled, squeezing even harder and making her winch. "Now get your ass in the car!" He barked, shoving her in the direction of the black parked stretch limo awaiting to leave.

She stumbled and tried desperately to catch her balance but failed miserably. She landed hard onto her right knee, skinning it and the palms of her hands against a headstone embedded in the grass.

Hal's six-foot frame towered above her.

"That's where I like to see you ... on your knees!" He sneered.

Jessica lowered her head and tried to control the rage surging beneath the surface. Slowly, she breathed in long, cleansing breaths to calm the quivering in her stomach. He was a man no one denied, as she gazed up at his hulking physique.

But she would outsmart him, and that she did, as she flipped about, pulled off her veil and threw it to the ground, and growled. "You disgusting pig. Takes a <u>real</u> <u>man</u> to beat up on a woman a quarter of his size."

She hated the smug look planted on his face and how he stood there all arrogant with his arms crossed at his chest.

"You goading me, little lady?"

Jessica's reaction was immediate, as she drew both of her knees to her chest and kicked out forcibly, hitting him square in the shins.

"Yep!" She replied matter-of-factly and laughed aloud as he tumbled backwards.

Jessica bolted to her feet, chuckling delightedly, as she watched him land with a splat into a mud puddle.

"Your days of telling me what to do are over, old man," she yelled.

"Hal!" Lorraine screamed, darting from the limousine. "Oh, my God! Jessica, what's wrong with you?"

Lorraine bent down and tried unsuccessfully to aid lifting him, grasping him under his arms.

"It's … okay … dear," she grunted, as she tugged upward. "Jessica didn't mean it. She's just upset that's all."

Lorraine's frustration was evident, as she began to slip and slide in the mix of mud and wet leaves. Her tone became aggravated. "Help a little, dear! I can't … lift you … by myself," she moaned, as she struggled to maintain her balance.

Hal's roar echoed through the cemetery, as he pushed her away with one backward swoop of his right arm.

Lorraine whirled out of control and squeaked in shocked horror, as she too landed onto her derriere into another shallow puddle. Globs of wet mud hung from her perfectly coiffed up-do and muddied her Christian Dior ensemble.

"Back off, you stupid bitch!" Hal barked. "If I want your goddamn help, I'll ask for it!"

Lorraine's hand flew to her mouth, and she gasped loudly, mud smearing across her cheek and the bridge of her nose. The chauffeur stood beside the stretch limousine frozen in his own shocked horror. He knew better than to intercede and offer his assistance. It took a few moments for her to rise with all the grace and dignity she could muster, and retreat to the car without speaking a word.

Jessica took a few safe steps backwards and watched as Hal rolled to his side.

"I gotta give it to you … you've got balls," he chuckled as he rose on one knee. "Men die for less."

Jessica tried not to show the fear that began to rumble deep in her belly. Yes, she was gutsy, but she knew danger … what it looked like, smelled like, and felt like.

"Another threat?" She retorted. "You may own this frigging town, but you no longer have a claim on me. When I leave here, I will no longer carry the Wilton name. That dies too, just like your son … the son you killed rearing him in your "ALMIGHTY" image."

Hal stepped forward, his face burning red from the fury she invoked.

She took a stance and stared him down.

Hal did not move. His chest heaved from the anger raging inside of him. He shifted his weight and rose to his full height, as he wiped his palms caked with thick, wet, mud upon his navy, Armani, pin-striped suit. He took a pure silk handkerchief from his breast pocket and slowly wiped the tiny splatters of mud from his face.

"We'll meet again?" He snarled through clenched teeth. "And when you least expect it," he continued, tossing his soiled linen to the ground and rubbed his hands together. "No one walks away from Hal Wilton unless I deem it so."

She grunted and sent him a disgusted look.

"Really? I don't think so. What about my Aunt?" She jibed smugly. "You know the lady ... Florence Rochelle Newcombe. I believe she's bested you more times than you care to admit. Touch me and she'll destroy you."

If looks could kill, Jessica would have turned to dust from the maniacal glare he sent her way. His nostrils flared, and a red flush slowly colored his neck and cheeks. He looked like a pressure cooker ready to blow its top.

But oh, how she relished the moment! Her eyes sparkled with admiration as her Aunt's face came to view in her mind's eye. What a woman Florence was ... all five feet six of her. She was full of vim and vigor with a regal grace and beauty that still left men breathless, when she entered a room. And how her amber eyes would sparkle like flames when her dander was up!

Yep! She thought. *Aunt Florence was one hell of a woman, who brought worse than him to their knees.* She smiled.

Hal could not hold a candle to her Aunt. Foreign heads of State, titled dignitaries and leading philanthropists held her in the highest regard. Furthermore, Hal knew Florence had the power and means to crush him like an ant.

Jessica could literally see the wheels churning in his over-inflated brain. She could not help but laugh out loud. Truth very seldom disarmed a man, but in this instance, it cut clear to the bone. She enjoyed her moment. Maybe she was wrong not confiding in her Aunt about Richard's abuse and his father's attempts to bed her. But once she did tell Florence, God hath no fury like her Aunt and God <u>help</u> Hal Wilton.

Florence had quite a dynasty to attend, especially since her husband passed away after

Jessica was married. Jessica just did not have the heart to burden Florence with her own problems. But it was different now.

Hal's eyes closed to reptilian slits. He seethed, as his chest rose and fell rapidly.

Despite her newfound courage, Jessica knew she let loose the devil. He was no longer family, but a predator out to devour her.

"You think you know me well enough to mock me?" He barked as he slowly circled his left shoulder a few times to test its flexibility.

Jessica retreated a few more steps, keeping her eyes locked on her adversary.

"I know vermin when I see it." She answered softly, standing her ground. "I am not your property. Threaten all you like. I'm leaving."

His eyes never wavered, never left hers, as he contemplated a moment longer.

Seconds passed. She was certain he wouldn't pounce, for it would show weakness on his part, and that wasn't Hal. He had thugs to do his dirty work for him. Still, her nerves felt as tight as the strings on a violin.

Hal stroked his chin, as he continued to stare her down. He took a quick step forward and halted.

Jessica could not help, but gasp slightly and she hated the look of confidence it gave him.

"Don't ever drop your guard, little lady," he sneered, circling around her and licking his lower lip in a disgusting manner.

Jessica made a face, and he snapped his teeth loudly at her and then roared with laughter.

"You'll never know when <u>daddy</u> will strike again."

Jessica felt repulsed by his lewd gesture and cringed. The urge to strike out and leave her handprint on his tanned cheek was overwhelming, but she controlled the impulse.

"Your day will come, mark my words. And I pray to God, it's before your son's body rots in his grave!"

Her tongue lashing did not faze him. Instead, he roared with laughter, as he turned and headed towards his awaiting limo.

CHAPTER TWO

She watched as the stretch limo turned the corner, before she began her three-block walk home. She needed to walk, to clear her head and think out a plan of action. She turned one last time to gaze over her shoulder at Richard's grave. The caretakers had already begun to remove the rich, colorful floral arrangements. She watched as one of them kicked a button with the toe of his boot and the casket slowly began to drop below ground level.

"Goodbye, Richard," she whispered softly, "if only you ..."

A sob caught in her throat. "If only" meant nothing at this point, she thought. She had closure, and it was time to move on and leave her past behind. She stepped forward, not looking back, and walked past the stones and soft hills of the small parish cemetery. Rows upon rows of stately elms, with crowns adorned in vivid golds, reds, and browns painted a beautiful autumn picture. A feeling of serene calmness came over her and she raised her face to let the light, misty rain wet her face.

Jessica took her time walking the tree-lined avenues of Wilton, trying to make sense of what had transpired over the past three days. In one horrific moment, she had been granted a reprieve, and set free from a domestically violent marriage.

She rubbed the palm of her hand over her cheek. It was still sore and tender from the vicious beating her husband administered before he died. She did not care anymore, who saw the bruises. She had nothing to be ashamed of. It was over now and time for her to move on and create a new life for herself.

Each step brought her closer to home and she began to feel a sense of renewed hope. There was no way she wanted to stay in Wilton. The small Maine town reeked of the corruption and intimidation of the family, who laid claim to it. She quickened her pace, and her steps were as light as her heart. As soon as she could, she would call her Aunt and make plans to leave. If anyone could help her make a fresh start, Florence could. Jessica smiled, when she thought of Albany, where she had the fondest of memories, growing up as a child.

Her Aunt's face came to mind once again. Even after losing her Uncle Ian, Florence had carried on his name and became a paramount force in Albany's financial arena. The Newcombe Dynasty was primary to revolutionizing Albany as a competitive port of commerce and strengthening its prominent stance as a leading capitol city on the East coast.

As she turned onto Sherman Lane, her level of anxiety to see and work with the handsome senator from New York increased. The Cape Cod home she once shared with Richard came into view. Jessica could not believe what a picture-perfect home it portrayed despite what happened behind its closed doors.

The yellow police taping protecting the crime scene had been removed and the diamond-glass windowpanes gleaned from the streaks of sun beginning to break through the dissipating grey clouds.

She entered and walked straight to the kitchen and poured herself a glass of Pinot. The sooner she talked to her Aunt, the quicker she could leave this life behind her. She settled upon the settee in front of the parlor window with her hand-crocheted afghan spread upon her lap and picked up her iPhone. She needed to see her Aunt's face, as well as hear her voice, and dialed her cell to 'FaceTime'.

In three rings, the line was answered, and her Aunt's face was visible.

"I hate that I wasn't there for you," her Aunt remarked immediately. "You look haggard, dear. My god! Is that bruising on your cheek? Jessica, what haven't you told me?"

Jessica took a long sip, placed her glass upon the coffee table in front of her, and sighed deeply, shaking her head.

"It's a long story, Aunt Florence. It's over. He can't hurt me anymore."

Her Aunt's look was not one of satisfaction, and when she opened her month to demand more than what Jessica wanted to offer, Jessica waved her hand to forestall her as a rush of emotion overwhelmed her.

Jessica did not know what came over her, as her reaction was immediate and all-consuming. It generated from the very depths of her soul and made her stomach lurch. She could not catch her breath or stop the faucet of tears that spilled over. Absently, she wiped them away, as she chewed her lower lip, trying to maintain some semblance of control. It did not work.

The stress, and agony, and fear, and abuse, and inability to fight back for more than a year had taken its toll. As hard as she tried to stall sobs, she simply could not and cried a river of tears.

Her Aunt did not interrupt and let her be. Jessica noted the silent tears streaming down her Aunt's face along with her. God! How she wished she were there right now just to be held in the comfort of her arms.

It had been so very long before anyone held her, caressed her, comforted and loved her. She hated showing weakness. She had always been a strong woman, but there was only so much she could take day-after-day without any show of support. If it hadn't been for Father Mulcahy, she would have caved in a long time ago.

She tried to control her sobs and sucked two, long cleansing breaths in and slowly released them. She hadn't cried, since the accident and found she still couldn't still the emotion that she held in for months. Her shoulders shook, as the agony of the last three days seeped from her pores. She craved the physical presence of her Aunt, needed the comfort of her embrace and her strong countenance to help her prevail.

The only solace her Aunt could offer was her silence, to let her cry, let the torment escape, that she had kept locked inside for so long.

"It's been utter hell," she managed to share and hiccupped.

"I expected as much, dear," her Aunt interrupted. "But enough now. Spilling tears over that despicable young man and that family … well, they don't deserve it! Do you hear me?" Her voice demanded.

Jessica sniffled and replied ever-so-softly, "Aha."

"Good," Florence replied. "Now ... I want you to pack just a few of your things. Leave everything else. There is nothing else you need from there. It's over. I'll send the jet. Martin and I will meet you at the airport," she called out for her butler and chauffeur. "Martin ... Martin! Hold on for a moment, dear, while I get Martin to help me with this."

Jessica watched, as her Aunt placed her cell down and moved away, still calling for her butler, who was more like family, having been of service for nearly twenty years. Jessica drew in a slow steady breath again to calm her quivering nerves.

Florence was right. There was nothing more she could do, or wanted. Wilton was never her home, as much as she tried to desperately make it so. She could hear her Aunt's footsteps and saw her smiling face, as she picked up her cell.

"You're all set, Jessica. The jet will arrive at Bangor Airport tomorrow at 7:45 a.m. and will fuel up right away. You should be in the air by 8:30. Remember, just bring a few things. We can buy whatever else you need once you're here. I love you, dear … very much. Let me help you get back on track and start anew. Do you remember Sen. Gallagher?" Her Aunt didn't give her a chance to reply, as she continued. "Well, he remembered you, as brief as that meeting was. He very much wants to talk to you about the vacant position in his office. He desperately needs someone and right away."

Jessica couldn't help but whimper, "Oh, Aunt Florence! What would I do without you? Thank you. Yes, please let the Senator know I can't wait to do just that."

"No need for thanks, Jessica. I love you like a daughter and can't wait to have you back home. See you tomorrow, dear. Now go pack and rest up."

Jessica blew her Aunt a kiss and ended the connection, letting loose a deep sigh of relief. Her Aunt's encouraging words of support gave her a sense of renewed hope. She felt rejuvenated, as if she could conquer anything … even escaping the clutches of her controlling father-in-law. She looked at her wristwatch. It was too early for dinner, but she had not eaten all day. She went to the kitchen and scrambled about for something quick to prepare and managed enough ingredients for a small salad and sandwich.

Once her belly was full, she knew that lying down for a nap was not an option and decided on a long hot shower instead, and turned, climbing the stairs to the second floor.

***

The hot, pulsating water from the shower head massaged her aching muscles like the fingers of a masseuse. Jessica rested her forehead against the shower wall. She could feel the tenseness in her shoulders relax, as the water drummed on her flesh. The strain of the day's events slowly melted away and she moaned blissfully.

Her skin glowed a soft pink, and as she scrubbed herself dry, she opened the door leading into the master bedroom. She jumped and shrieked with fright when she noted Hal standing in her room. Her eyes darted to the window. It had to be the only way he could have entered, and then she realized it was closed and they were two floors up.

"How the hell did you get in here?" She bellowed, gripping her bath towel tighter about her nakedness.

Dear God! The look of ravenous hunger reflected in his eyes struck the worse fear deep in the pit of her stomach. She could feel the nausea slowly rise in her throat and looked about quickly for a means of escape, but there was none. She was trapped, and she gulped fretfully as she side-stepped to the left. His stare was intense, as he gawped at the soft swell of her breasts peeking out above her towel. She adjusted it quickly and side-stepped again, when he moved forward, reaching out for her.

He raised his other hand, swinging a key on a single ring, with a self-assured look, that pissed her off.

Her eyes flamed with hatred. "Where do you get off coming here like this?"

Hal sprinted forward, and his fingers grazed along the curve of her shoulder.

Jessica slapped his hand away, dove for the bed and rolled clear to the other side. Her breasts rose and fell, as she fought to quell the fear threatening to consume her.

Hal's gate was slow and deliberate, and his eyes gleaned with destructive intent. "Aw come on. I think it's time you show a little thanks for everything I've paid for all this time."

Jessica wanted nothing more than to slash his handsome face to shreds.

"You, bastard! Have you no remorse? You just buried your son, and now you're trying to bed his widow. You're pure evil!" She spat vehemently.

Hal smirked and placed a knee atop the mattress.

He waved her comment off, as though it were trivial and replied. "He was worthless and careless."

Jessica knew he wasn't a man to take lightly. Despite his sixty-four years, his money helped keep him lean and hard of muscle. He was a devout runner and worked out daily with a private trainer. Except for the distinguished grey coloring his temples, one would think him to be a man in his early fifties.

She slowly moved backward, until she felt her nightstand grace the back of her knees. She reached behind and slowly retrieved a pair of scissors she had left lying there earlier after trimming her hair. As she watched him move his hand to his pant zipper, she held them like a hammer out in front of her, so she could draw them back and drive them into his gullet or slash out in any direction like an expert swordsman.

"I'd think twice if I were you. Take another step closer and I swear you'll regret it."

She barely took a breath, watching him closely, as he sized up the situation. His hand froze briefly, and he stared her down. She knew he was taking in the very sight of her. She could feel droplets of water fall from her wet hair and slowly slide down her skin and disappear between her firm breasts. She could not help but notice the bulge in his pants and how his tongue slowly grazed along his lower lip.

"God, you make me hard," he groaned.

She raised the scissors higher, and he took a step forward. "I mean it, Hal!"

Their eyes locked, chests heaving with shallow breaths, each summing up the other, wondering who would buckle first. Seconds passed, and minutes hung heavy in the air like a fog.

Hal crossed his arms and leaned against her four- poster.

"Haven't I taken care of you" He huffed, changing his tactic. "It pains me that you feel this way, Jessica. I mean … I've provided this beautiful cottage for you to live in, made sure my son had a generous income to keep you in the lap of luxury …"

Jessica shrieked.

"The lap ... are you kidding me!" She turned to her left and flung open the closet door. Dozens of empty hangars hung in a perfect row, except for a few slacks, blouses, one skirt, a day dress and denim shift. A pair of worn sneakers sat on the floor beneath the hangars, along with two pairs of black flats, dressy black pumps, and a light tan pair of winter boots.

"Do you see furs hanging here or an array of designer outfits?" She moved to her jewelry chest and dumped it atop her coverlet. "No precious gems, diamonds there either," she spat. "The only luxury you ever afforded was catering to your son's vices!"

Hal raised an eyebrow and smiled.

"Oh! Don't be so smug," she spewed. "The whores didn't bother me. I was glad he sated his sadistic hungers elsewhere."

"He wouldn't have looked elsewhere, if he got what was expected of you ..."

"You son of a bitch," she interrupted, as she lifted the edge of her towel to expose her upper thigh. "This is what he liked," she pointed with the scissors still in her hand. "Recognize them, Hal? Cigarette burns. Do you do that to those high-priced whores you bed? Did he learn that from you too?"

She was surprised by the horrified look on his face. She let the towel drop back into place and crossed her arms over her chest.

"I may have pulled the trigger, but you're the one, who killed him. You pampered and nurtured him to expect those less fortunate than him cater to his every whim. He drowned himself in alcohol, because he wanted to be like you. He had affairs with your leftovers. He was your carbon copy," she shook her head with a disgusted laugh. "The pitiful thing is, it made him a weak, ugly, vile little man just like you. I am so done. I don't need you, or this house," she waved. "Now get the hell out!"

Hal snickered. "What makes you think you've got a choice? You're still a Wilton, sweetheart."

"Don't threaten me, old man."

Hal pounced forward, and Jessica swiped the scissors upward, grazing his left cheek and drawing blood. He fell backwards and growled between clenched teeth, as he glared at the scissors still held between her hands, threatening contact again. He wiped away the blood running down his cheek with the back of his hand, then raised his palms in compliance, as if to calm her.

"Oh please. When are, you going to realize, I have a more positive force in my life ... the Newcombe Empire? That is my inheritance. I don't need you and despise everything you stand for."

The corner of her mouth lifted victoriously, as she watched the color drain from his face.

She had struck a chord, a wonderfully, splendorous chord.

"I know that's why you sought out my grandmother ... for a contract of marriage with your son. Did you really expect to control me, to gain access to my inheritance one day? Guess again."

The look of contempt he sent her confirmed her suspicions all along. Now she was more than certain, why he wanted her to stay on in Wilton, so he could control the empire her Aunt Florence would one day will to her.

"I'm bored with this little exchange," she waved. "I told you to leave, and I won't tell you again." She didn't want him privy to her plans to flee. "When my Aunt returns from Europe in a couple of weeks, I'm out of here."

She hoped she sounded convincing enough. She could not tell from the look on his face whether, or not, he believed her.

Hal scrunched his lips and nodded. "You're not the little mouse I thought my son married. I quite like that in you. Makes you more appealing ... worthier of the challenge."

More like prized game to be hunted and caged, she thought.

She knew he would not allow for her to leave. She could already see the wheels turning in his sick, depraved mind. She knew she had to move fast, and that meant now.

"I like a little adventure." He toyed, closing the distance between them.

She was trapped. She could feel the sheen of sweat on her skin and her pulse beating in her ears, as her heart pounded furiously in her chest. No matter where she moved, she could not get away. She held the scissors tightly in front of her, and ready to plunge the sharp sheers into his belly, if need be. Just when she expected him to pounce, he plopped down upon the edge of the bed and leaned back on his elbows.

"Look. I'm a fair man. I'll make it worth your while to stick around until I tire of you."

Her jaw dropped open and she just as quickly closed it. This man was relentless. The gall of him. To think he was that powerful to assume, whatever he offered, was worthy of considering and accepting.

"If it gets you the hell out of my house, yes, I'll bite," she cow-towed.

He laughed, and she knew he thought he won at wearing her down.

Let him think whatever he wants, she thought.

He clapped his hands and rose. "Now, that's more like it. I'll send a car tomorrow … dinner … 7 p.m. Wear something … alluring. Go to Mitzy's on Main and charge my account. I'm confident we can come to something amicable."

He moved toward the door, stopped and turned. "I wouldn't think of leaving, Jessica. You know how I get, when I'm disappointed."

Jessica sent him a smug smile. She could only imagine what his reaction would be, once he found her gone. She also would not put it past him to have a "watch" placed on her house. When Hal wanted something … someone, he went to great lengths to accomplish that goal, no matter who got hurt in the process, or stood in his way. She knew she could not wait until the next day to leave. Escaping now was paramount.

CHAPTER THREE

There was an unexplainable sense of unease that washed over Jessica, as she decided her next course of action. She did not know what it was, but she knew whatever it was, it was not good. She quickly moved to the bedroom window. It was no longer raining, and then, out of the corner of her eye, she detected movement.

There, in the shadows across the street, she saw a shadow, a figure of … a man. She focused her gaze more intently on the huge elm tree, and there it was, a large, black mass that did not belong there. And she knew. She was being watched. Her temper flares and her pulse quickened. She spread the curtains opened wide and looked in the opposite direction instead for a few brief moments, trying not to give her discovery away.

"Of all the nerve," she sputtered and slowly drew the shade all the way down. "He never ceases to amaze me."

She threw off her robe, threw on her sweats, and ran down the hallway toward the stairs. When she got to the kitchen, she went down on all fours and crawled to the back. Slowly, she rose to peer carefully out the bow window. She took her time scanning the area, looking for something out of place, another shadowy figure hiding in the darkness, and could not see anything out of the ordinary. She exhaled deeply her relief. She didn't want to take any chances, slid back down to the floor, and thought briefly what her next plan of action should be.

She rose and walked to the wall phone, removed it from the receiver, and stopped in mid-air. If Hal had a key to her house, she would not have put it past him to have her house phone tapped as well. She had no other option. She could not wait until morning to leave for the airport. She had to get out of town now.

She quickly exited the kitchen and went back to her bedroom to use her cell phone and dialed the local taxi service.

After she gave a fictitious name, the dispatcher assured her a driver would pick her up in twenty minutes out in front of the local variety store, which was only a block away. She gazed at the alarm clock on the nightstand beside her bed. It was almost nine. She hated the thought of sitting up all night at the airport, but it was clearly better than being spotted leaving in the light of day tomorrow.

Jessica hastened to prepare for her escape. She did not pack any of her belongings as planned, decided to dress herself entirely in black, pulled her hair up into a ponytail to let it dry naturally, drew the strap of her purse over her neck, and headed for the stairs.

Jessica managed to slip from the house through the back yard without being spotted. Quietly, she crossed her neighbor's yard and the next one over as well. Once she turned the corner onto Dover Court, she ran as fast as her legs could carry her. She could see the yellow taxi traveling towards her and pull up to the curb beside the Wilton Country Store. Her heart thundered in her chest, and she prayed the driver had the good sense to wait.

She was about to scream and flail her arms wildly to draw his attention until she noticed, Mr. Peterson, the elderly store manager exiting the store, and locking it up for the night. His eyes twinkled happily, as he peered over the rim of his wire spectacles, when she approached.

"How are you, young lady," he asked kindly, reaching out to tenderly pat the side of her arm. "I was so sorry to hear what happened to you dear and apologize for not attending the services," he admitted embarrassingly. "Mr. Wilton wouldn't let me close the store, you see and ..."

Jessica shook her head in reply. "No. No. Please. I truly understand," she leaned in and placed a soft kiss upon his wrinkled cheek.

Someone touched her shoulder from behind making her jump and said, "Going somewhere Mrs. Wilton?"

She could feel the color drain from her face and her heart skip a beat or two in fear of being found out.

"Land sakes, child! What's wrong? You're plum white!" Mr. Peterson asked, as he wrapped a protective arm about her shoulder with fatherly concern.

She slowly turned to face the person behind her and nearly fainted, when she realized it was not who she expected it might be, but rather, Mr. Hingle, the mailman.

The postman exclaimed with the deepest concern, "I truly am sorry, Mrs. Wilton! I didn't mean to startle you."

Jessica emitted a nervous laugh. "I guess I'm a little jittery. It's been a long, tiring day."

The gentleman nodded in agreement. "Well, no wonder, after what you've been through these past few days. May I walk you home? You sure are trembling a might."

Jessica raised her hands in protest and smiled. "No, no I'm fine. As a matter of fact, this is my taxi. Thank you though. I'm fine, really." She reached out and rubbed Mr. Peterson's arm lightly and smiled. "If you'll excuse me, I'm running late already and must be going."

Once she relaxed in the comfort of the taxi, she reflected on the numerous times the endearing manager had shown her kindness, when no one else would. Most of the inhabitants of Wilton lived in fear of her father-in-law. Their smiles never reached their eyes, except for the dear elderly manager. She used to love listening to his stories about Maine, especially since he was the state's historian for nearly four decades.

She always loved Maine. It was a popular vacation spot when she was a child. That was then. The memories that haunted her dreams now left an entirely different lasting impression.

***

Jessica was greeted by Captain McKenzie the moment she boarded her Aunt's private Gulfstream. It was a magnificent performance machine that exuded both excellence and grace.

He stood proudly before the cockpit, and she quickly glimpsed inside and felt wowed by the complex and cutting-edge controls and side-mounted displays that would be at the Captain's and co-pilot's fingertips. His warm welcoming smile made her feel instantly safe, and she was more anxious than ever to get into the air.

He tipped his cap and bowed slightly and welcomed her. "Good morning to you, Mrs. Wilton …"

"Jessica, please," she interrupted, as she accepted the hand he extended.

He nodded and continued as he released his grasp, "Jessica … welcome aboard. We're ready for takeoff, so please, make yourself comfortable. As soon as we level off, our hostess Allison," he pointed to a sweet, petite female entering from the aft section of the cabin, "will make sure your trip is a pleasurable one as well."

Allison extended her hand in welcome and smiled warmly. "It'll be my pleasure to serve you, Jessica." She turned and extended her arm, "please sit wherever you'd like, and as soon as we reach the proper altitude, I'll be serving a light breakfast."

Jessica moved forward and could not help but be both impressed and awed by the opulence of the cabin. It was approximately eight feet long and could comfortably sit about eighteen passengers. Allison let her know the cabin offered high-speed connectivity with a broadband multilink data system, wireless networking, onboard printing, and phone service should she need it.

The interior was decorated in soft earth tones with double-wide beige seats and couches made from the finest Italian leather and slick mahogany tables and sideboards. The technology provided touch-screen capability to control the cabin's temperature, lighting, window shades and varied entertainment options.

Huge oval-shaped windows were positioned higher on the fuselage to offer a panoramic view of the outside. Allison pushed a button embedded in the top right side of a long cabinet, that separated the cabin from the galley.

Jessica watched as a huge flat screen rose from inside the cabinet and slowly shook her head in amazement.

She settled into one of the wide single seats mid-way down the aisle and buckled herself in. She could hear Allison inform the Captain they were clear for takeoff. The engines immediately revved. The wheels slowly rolled the jet back out of its ramp, maneuvering onto the taxiway, and they were third in line for takeoff.

She felt as though a thousand pounds had been lifted from her shoulders. She got away, she smiled triumphantly. She was finally free. Despite the euphoria she felt accomplishing the feat, she still could not help, but feel remorse for her part in Richard's death. It bothered her terribly, regardless of the abuse and humiliation she was forced to endure. She knew her actions were justified. She knew she was a decent person. She knew she tried with all her might to salvage her marriage and beg Richard to get help.

But she also knew in her heart, that Richard would have killed her that night, if she had not defended herself. Her eyes filled with tears, as she reflected on all the painful memories that would hold her hostage for quite some time. And the greatest loss most of all, was the child Richard took from her.

Her hand absently reached for her mid-section, as she gazed mindlessly out the window and slowly massaged the area, that once cocooned the babe she lost almost six months ago.

There was nothing she could do then, despite her efforts to shield herself and safeguard the baby from his brutal attack. Tears streamed from her eyes, as she remembered the anguish and pain she bore and would haunt her for the rest of her life.

CHAPTER FOUR

The moment the wheels touched down on the runway, Jessica felt safe for the first time in what seemed forever. She could not wait to see her Aunt and get on with her new life. Once the plane neared its private hangar, she released the seat belt and noticed a shiny, black town car was parked to the side. Her Aunt's chauffeur, Martin, exited the car and opened the back door. Jessica's eyes filled with tears, when her Aunt exited the vehicle and turned her gaze toward the plane.

Her Aunt's broad smile sent a feeling of calmness to wash over her, and Jessica waved excitedly from the window. The hostess, Allison, let Jessica know she was clear to disembark the plane and Jessica popped out of her seat quickly. Patiently, she waited for Allison to unlock the cabin door. Jessica thanked the captain and hostess graciously, stepped over the threshold, and immediately descended the steps.

She watched as her Aunt walked briskly forward to greet her, and Jessica quickened her steps to close the gap between them. It was an emotional reunion, as they both broke into tears and wrapped their arms tightly about each other, plying each other's cheeks with tender kisses, and speaking words of endearment.

Her Aunt held her at arm's length and looked her over with a critical eye.

"You look ghastly, dear. Whatever have they done to you?" Her Aunt looked behind her and her gaze was puzzled. "No luggage?"

Jessica shook her head. "No, none … just what you see here," she lifted the purse from her shoulder and pointed to her clothing. "I was being watched and had to move quickly."

Florence sent her a look that made her gulp.

"Did he threaten you, that bastard?"

Jessica sighed deeply. "That, and more." She looped her arm through her Aunt's and directed her toward the town car. "I'll fill you in on the way, okay?"

She focused her attention on Martin and extended her hand in greeting.

"Hello, Martin. It's good to see you again."

He was ever-so gracious as he bowed respectfully, before taking her hand tenderly between his big, brawny ones, speaking softly.

"Tis very good to see you too, Miss Jessie, and welcome home. It'll be a pleasure serving you once again."

A tender smile crossed her lips as she replied. "Martin, you're a dear and the feeling is mutual I assure you. Will you go riding with me again?" She winked playfully. She knew from his reaction that her question pleased him.

"I'm serious, Martin. I won't ride with anyone, but you."

There was a sentimental softness that shone in his eyes, as he smiled warmly and planted a fatherly kiss upon her brow. "I'm touched and would love nothing more." He stepped toward the back door and opened it for them to enter, closed it, when they were both seated comfortably inside, and moved to the driver side, entering.

Just as the town car pulled away, her Aunt turned to her with a look of determination planted upon her face. Jessica knew what she was going to ask before the words slipped from her Aunt's lips. She knew that Florence would be livid, but for her own safety, Jessica knew it would not be wise to hold anything back. She lifted her hand to forestall her Aunt's words and inhaled deeply before she began to tell her about Hal and his offer.

"He what?" Her Aunt bellowed. "How dare he imply that you … that a Rochelle take to his bed like a paid whore! Did he touch you … force you? You must tell me, Jessica."

Jessica shook her head in the negative, and her Aunt continued her rave.

"His day will come, dear. That, I promise you. He will sorely pay. But we will have that conversation some other time. I'm sure you must be famished and can't wait to soak in a nice hot bath."

"Yes, I am and would love nothing more," she replied.

The twenty-minute drive was relaxing, as her Aunt told her of the changes made around the estate, what had been going on in Albany's social arena, and her latest conversations with Sen. Gallagher about Jessica coming on board. She listened intently and began to relax. A sense of peace washed over her, and for the first time, she felt safe.

"As soon as Clora is done fussing over you, I'll send her out with Martin to pick up some necessary items you'll need. Tomorrow we'll make a day of it and do some shopping if you'd like. I can't remember when the last time was, I had the pleasure of going on a spree. It'll be fun. What do you think dear?" She patted her thigh lightly.

Jessica gave her Aunt an affectionate hug and kiss. "Oh, Aunt Florence. I've missed you so, so much. I'd be happy in rags, as long as, we were together, forever."

"Well, that's sweet, Jessica. But a woman like you, deserves happiness and the love of a good man. It would be delightful introducing you to those young men I, in fact, know are worthy of your attention, and your heart."

Jessica leaned her head against her Aunt's shoulder and sighed disparagingly.

"Oh, Aunt Florence. I am so done with men. I thought I had married the greatest catch in all of Maine. It just isn't right how a man of such fine breeding can turn out to be so deranged. Let's hold off on that for a while, o.k.?" She gazed up at her Aunt lovingly. "I do love you though for the thought."

Florence caressed her cheek with her palm and smiled before replying.

"I'll not let you wallow for too long. That beast of a husband of yours does not deserve your sorrow. The holidays will be soon upon us and I'm a festive woman. You've got until then."

Jessica couldn't help, but chuckle. Her Aunt was right and there was no sense arguing with her, because she knew in her heart, Florence was just the person she needed to help her get on with her life.

The wide waterway they began to cross was the Hudson River, separating the Counties of

Albany and Rensselaer. There were so many changes, since the last time she was home. Two more lanes in both directions had been added to the interstate to accommodate the ever-growing traffic. They drove past new community developments with homes priced in the mid-two-hundred thousand range, a brand-new elementary school, multiple strip malls, mega movie theatre, and a new Christian church, that looked more like an arena.

A massive Nano Technology Complex had been constructed in her absence, that stood impressive beside the Albany skyline, spanning acres with buildings five levels high encased in steel and impenetrable dark green glass.

It was a new Albany, and she rather liked it that way. As she was beginning a new chapter in her life, it made it seem all rather adventurous rediscovering her old stomping grounds all over again. Jessica realized this was the beginning of many new and wondrous changes in her life. For a long time, decisions weren't her own. Every day she was told what to do, how to dress, who she could talk to, and what was expected of her. Freedom was going to take some time getting used to, and she welcomed it greedily.

The town car made a right onto a private road and Jessica's breath caught in her throat, as she gazed in wonderment at the beautiful landscape before her. The modest estate was every bit elegant, and as they approached the circular driveway, the stately English brick colonial came into view, set off by three majestic, white pillars.

The grounds encompassing her Aunt's estate, were an array of manicured lawns, shrubs, varied pines of blue spruce, Douglas fir and hemlock; and an abundance of flower gardens of every color, style, and fragrance.

All Jessica could do was gasp.

"It is beautiful, isn't it, dear?" Florence asked. "I feel the same way every time Martin pulls into the driveway. I sooo love this house."

Jessica didn't have a chance to answer as Florence's housekeeper, Clora, exited the front door, squealing with delight.

"Miss Jessie, you is home, child. Praise the Lord," she clapped her hands joyously and opened her arms wide to receive her. She embraced Jessica to her robust bosom and crooned.

"It sure is good to see you child, after all this time. And you is all skin and bones," she scorned, as she turned Jessica about for inspection, clucking her tongue in dismay. "Clora is gonna have to plump you up, and there is no better time than the present. Um um um," she hummed, shaking her head. "The table is all set, and da food is waiting for consumption." She wrapped a possessive arm about Jessica's waist and led her into the foyer, leaving her mistress of the house and butler to chuckle and follow from behind.

Jessica looked over her shoulder at her Aunt and Martin, smiling as she watched Martin offer her Aunt his arm.

"Well, Martin, shall we?" Her Aunt waved toward the entrance. "Join us please, won't you for something to eat, in celebration of Jessie's return."

He placed her hand in the curve of his arm, escorting her towards the front door and replied.

"I would be most happy too. This old house is smiling upon us, Mrs. Newcombe. It's good to have her home, once again."

Clora had outshone herself, as she beautifully set a table befitting a king's honor. A duck had been roasted to a golden brown and served with a delicate orange sauce. The crab for the salad had been flown in fresh that day.

Florence ordered a special wine from her cellar collection to celebrate the occasion. Once dinner was on the table, Martin and Clora joined them to partake in the feast.

It was a glorious reunion. The last time they had been together was just shortly after her engagement was announced. They honored and respected the pain she had been through and no discussion of her husband Richard, or his death, was brought up at the table. Jessica loved how her Aunt included her staff to partake in special family celebrations. Martin and Clora had been in her Aunt's employ ever since she was an infant. They were more than hired help. They were extended family.

Once dessert was finished, the table was cleared and everyone retired to the sitting room, where a warm fire was already ablaze in the large fieldstone fireplace. Brandy sifters were passed around and a final toast to good health and happiness was made. Martin and

Clora graciously retired for the evening, so Jessica and her Aunt could spend some time alone.

The warmth that emitted from the blazing flames, the crackling sounds of the logs as they burned, and the slow hissing of the moisture being drawn from the wood was inviting. Jessica settled back into a thickly-tufted oversized chair and sighed contentedly.

"It's so good to be back home, Aunt Florence."

"I've missed you too, dear."

A moment of silence passed between them. She could not help but think of the child she had lost, and her palm slowly moved over her lower abdomen. She ached for that feeling of movement, that was no longer there. If only she could have gotten away sooner, she thought, her daughter would have had the chance to survive and be born into a safe, healthy, and happy environment.

My darling, sweet, little girl ... my Suzanne.
I'm so sorry I couldn't protect you.

She swallowed the lump in her throat, and it constricted painfully, as she tried desperately to hold back the tears. She wanted to tell her Aunt about Suzanne, about how she lost her, about what Richard had done. She couldn't. She hadn't the strength to relive that horror also again.

As a tear escaped, she quickly wiped it away. She forced herself to think of something else. She couldn't let that painful loss drag her back down, down into that dark pit of nothingness she had escaped to, when she didn't eat, didn't talk, hadn't bathed and wallowed for weeks, after her loss. It had taken everything she was ... to push herself ... to move on.

It was then, she remembered, that when she was a young girl, she would sit and listen to her Aunt tell stories of their family's history in this very same room. She realized, she wanted to hear those stories again more than ever. She needed to be reconnected to that person she once was, to reconfirm where she came from, who her ancestors were, the proud heritage that made her the woman she had become and had lost for quite some time.

"Tell me the stories, please."

Her Aunt looked puzzled as she repeated Jessica's request. "The stories, dear?"

"When I was younger … you know … about our family. Please. I need … "

She swallowed back the urge to cry, as her voice shook with emotion. "I just need to hear them again."

Florence nodded knowingly and took a short sip of her brandy.

"Of course, dear. Should I start from the beginning?"

Jessica nodded her reply.

"Let me see now," Florence paused briefly, as she gathered her thoughts and shortly began in a soft, soothing voice.

"When colonization became brisk, the Dutch West India Company was given a nice monopoly of American trade. Under its direction, Dutch merchants established friendly relations with the powerful Iroquois tribes, who welcomed them as potential allies against the French, occupying the St. Lawrence Valley. The trading company had maintained posts as far up the Hudson River at Fort Orange, which later became the city of Albany.

It was at this post, Jessica, our history was born. Your great, great, great grandfather, Colonel Gerard Rochelle was the commanding officer at the Fort. Oh, he was such a resourceful and handsome young man!"

Jessica's gaze met the portrait that hung on the far wall of the sitting room. He was indeed a very striking man, with eyes the same color green as hers, looking back at her.

"Your grandfather won the immediate friendship of the territorial natives and responsible for protecting the mixed colonies of Dutch, French, and Swedish settlers. Quite the crisis had begun to develop when the English began to settle into the Mohawk Valley. They were a terrible lot, invading the hunting grounds of the Iroquois. The Indians had long been friendly with them, but it was feared such an insult would cause them to desert to France's side, leaving them without a powerful ally.

So, the Board of Trade assembled a congress at Albany in 1754. It was attended by representatives from New York, Pennsylvania, Maryland, and the New England colonies. And my dear, because of the high esteem your grandfather was held by both red and white men alike, he was honored to represent New York at the young age of thirty-two."

Jessica welled with pride. She had forgotten she was made of such fine stock. Being under the Wilton's thumb for so long, and victim to their barrage of insults and abuse, had lessened her self-esteem over time. It had been a terrible struggle. Despite how strong of a person she knew she was, it was difficult trying to decide whether she should end her marriage. Her ambivalence was confusing … whether to stay or go … whether things would get better … whether Richard might change. It was like her Aunt knew what she was thinking at that moment.

"You come from greatness, Jessica. Your grandfather met the love of his life at that time, Florence Livingston, whom I'm named after. There has been a Rochelle representative at New York's Legislature, up until your dad was killed in that terrible accident. Don't ever question your worth, your strength, or your ability, dear … never again."

Jessica pondered her words briefly, before she responded.

"When Grandma Rochelle raised me, she never spoke much about my mom and dad. Everything I know, is because of you. My dad must have been quite the Senator, hah?"

Her Aunt nodded and smiled wistfully, as she too reflected for a moment.

"My brother was something else, yes. His constituents and colleagues adored him. He would have never let you enter into such a marriage either." She waved her finger matter-of-factly. "I hate to say it, but our mother was a conniving and manipulative woman. All she cared about was money and status. The way she misguided you, was unforgiveable."

She watched as her Aunt rose and added another log onto the fire. She bent over to stoke the coals first, then placed the log over them. She rose and turned with a broad smile upon her face, as though she had some big secret to share.

"What are you thinking?" Jessica coaxed. "You're up to something. I can tell."

Her Aunt laughed heartily, as she seated herself and took another sip from her glass of brandy.

"Nothing really, dear. You're going to fit in nicely with Bryan's team. I just know it. It'll be wonderful seeing a Rochelle back at the Capitol again."

"I'm a little nervous about that. What if he doesn't hire me? It's been, my god ages, since I've conversed with people on such an intellectual level. Richard kept me prisoner, Aunt Florence. I rarely got out."

Her Aunt waved her remark off. "Oh pooh. You graduated from Berkeley with honors in communications. He'll hire you, and, you'll assimilate just fine. Besides, by the time I give you some inside pointers, you'll be one step ahead of those dimwits, who used bed sheets instead of brains and experience, to get their jobs."

"Well, alright then. You've convinced me just fine." She couldn't hold back a long yawn that rose from nowhere and she chuckled lightly. "Sorry. Suddenly, I feel so drained. I guess we should call it an evening?"

"I'd say that's a good idea." Florence rose and closed the distance between them. Together they walked arm-in-arm out of the room and up to the second floor, where they bid each other a good night with warm embraces and sweet kisses.

The suite of rooms, which Jessica would use as her own, were tastefully decorated in soft floral shades of pink and grey. It overlooked one of the larger flower gardens adorned with American beauty roses. There was a window seat, where she could comfortably stretch out.

It was lavished with the plumpest of pillows. Her bed was a queen size canopy covered with a quilted soft green satin comforter, dusted with pink and grey throw pillows of various shapes and sizes.

There was a private bath for her personal use, with a sunken Jacuzzi tub big enough to fit three people. The walk-in closet could fit a twin sized bed comfortably, and she knew that her Aunt would forcibly persuade her to fill it to capacity. She was thankful for her Aunt. Now that she was truly home, she knew that eventually her life would take on some sense of normalcy. She moved toward the window seat and knelt on her knees, leaning forward to open the window a little.

A soft breeze drifted in, along with those evening sounds that were calming and peaceful. The garden looked even more beautiful, indirectly aglow with soft lighting. She heard the distant hoot of an owl, the chirping of crickets, the croak of a few frogs that took up residence in the pond off to the left of the garden, where water cascaded from the fountain placed there to keep the water circulating. She was glad the estate was located far enough from the city. She enjoyed living in the country.

Her mind began to drift, and the shadows shifted as the scene before her changed, and she began to reminisce the past, and view the outside through the eyes of a young woman just eighteen back in Maine.

She was at her grandmother's summer home on Mt. Desert Island, one of the most beautiful on the Atlantic Coast. It was dotted with refined, stately summer homes, like her grandmothers.

The only way one could reach the rugged, granite mainland was by a short bridge, where the beauty of forested, flowered bays and inlets could be seen, always brightly colored by sails of boats that skimmed the horizon.

It was that summer she was introduced to Richard, heir to the Wilton Empire. She did not know then a contract of marriage had been arranged. He knew though. He was adept and experienced with women. She was a virgin, naïve, and intent on her studies, even during Summer break. He played havoc with her feelings, inciting emotions she had never felt and could barely reign in.

He was expert at creating a fire deep inside of her, stirring a desire with hot, lingering kisses and passionate ministrations that dulled her senses and left her wanton and craving more.

By the time Fall had arrived, they were the talk of Maine. When he proposed, it was magical. Musicians serenaded as they danced beneath a twinkling night sky. They walked barefoot along a moonlit beach, listening to the tranquil sound of waves crashing along the shoreline. When he avowed his love, and offered marriage, she had believed him with all of her heart.

Theirs was a Cinderella wedding. Her gown, which was designed in Paris, was an elegant, white satin. The yoke and collar were kissed with tiny pearls and sequin-embroidered Schiffli lace. The sleeves were luxuriously fitted and the bodice was covered in pearls and tiny Swarovski crystals.

The reception was grand, attended by the most influential of guests. A private jet took the newlyweds to the Greek Isles, and on the third day of their blissful getaway, the horror began.

A single tear trickled down her cheek as flashes of the mental and physical abuse she had endured, flitted behind her tightly closed eyes.

How he could have been so sinister … so heartless, would forever remain a mystery, forever buried with him back in St. Augustine's cemetery.

Her eyes popped open and she wiped the tears staining her cheeks away with the heel of her palms.

Enough! It's over. Your free … free to live life as you may.

It would still take a while, for her to believe the words, that echoed in her mind.

CHAPTER FIVE

Florence's idea of shopping was short of mind-boggling. Jessica's head spun over the numerous designer storefronts that graced one city block of Manhattan's garment district. She argued profusely with her Aunt, when she realized where they were headed. She never paid more than twenty dollars for a pair of sneakers or heels, and the thought of her Aunt dishing out thousands for anything attached to a designer label was beyond ludicrous.

She should have known better, though. Her Aunt knew how to find amazing deals on designer apparel with sample sales. Florence knew where to go to purchase high-end merchandise at a fraction of the cost. They shopped for nearly three days, until she was fitted with an adequate wardrobe suitable for casual, formal and nighttime wear.

It seemed weird to be treated as a tourist. Living in the Capitol Region most of her life, one would assume she would have gotten to visit the 'Big Apple' at some point, but no. It just never happened. Her grandmother kept her cloistered away at a boarding school further upstate, until she graduated from high school and then, she took up residence at Berkeley another four years.

She was held spellbound as they toured the entire city over the next four days. They took their time and walked the financial district, revering over some of the most uniquely, architecturally designed buildings. She loved their carriage ride through Central Park and adored Broadway, where her Aunt purchased balcony tickets for the showing of 'Chicago'.

Jessica couldn't get enough of the sights and sounds of the City; the fog rolling in over the

East River, the street-side vendors and performers, the numerous colorful flags, gracing the United Nations Building, the stoic, yet gracefully beautiful lady standing proud on Liberty Island and the ever-impressive Metropolitan Museum of Art, where they spent an entire day goggling over the exhibits that spanned multiple cultures and decades of time periods.

Her Aunt maintained a suite of rooms for them during their stay at the Waldorf-Astoria on Park Avenue. Jessica loved it, because it was a well-kept relic of the past. Time honored, as it was, it still held title as one of Manhattan's finest.

No city in the world either, had as many fine restaurants, serving a multitude of national dishes, as New York. Eating here was an adventure, as she tested her taste buds with dishes she normally would have snubbed her nose at.

She was readying herself for bedtime, when her Aunt called out to her and knocked on the door connecting their rooms.

"Are you decent dear?"

"Come in, Aunt Florence."

Her Aunt entered, breathless from the overly large package she was carrying, which was beautifully wrapped with a soft pink satin bow.

"Is that for me!" Jessica exclaimed.

"Yes, it is," her Aunt replied. "Do you remember the Maurice Levkoff boutique we visited the other day and chose an evening dress for you?"

"That's it," Jessica squealed happily. "They've altered it already?"

Jessica retrieved the box from her Aunt and hurriedly placed it atop her bed and began to unwrap the bow.

"I asked them to rush it, dear. I was anxious for you to have it for tomorrow."

Jessica paused lifting the top off the package, as she exchanged a puzzled look with her Aunt.

"Why tomorrow?"

"Well, there's a gala at the Met, and I thought it would be the perfect opportunity for you to get your feet wet."

Jessica chewed at her lower lip and hesitated to lift the top off the dress box.

"So soon?"

Her Aunt waved her hand at the box for her to hurry along.

Jessica lifted the lid, let the top slip to the floor, pulled back the sheer tissue paper and gaped openly as a whish escaped her lips.

"Have you ever seen anything so exquisite?" She purred, as she lifted the creation from the box, held it in front of her and slowly twirled before the full-length floor mirror in awe of the reflection gazing back at her.

"No dear," her Aunt replied. "I do believe it is <u>the</u> most ravenous gown I've ever seen."

The undergarment was royal blue satin of mid-calf length, set off by a cloak of white Schiffli embroidery, with mid-length scalloped sleeves and matching hemline, delicately stitched with tiny, intricate rosebuds and belted with a `royal blue silk ribbon.

"I think I may have to hire a bodyguard to keep all the young bucks in this City at bay and the single women from killing you over pure jealousy," her Aunt chuckled.

Jessica made a face and clucked at her Aunt. "I admit the dress is simply beautiful, but I don't believe men will be throwing themselves at my feet, Aunt Florence."

Her Aunt plopped down on the edge of her bed, shaking her head in argument.

"You've been sheltered too long, child. I truly believe you have no clue what a natural beauty you are. Your arrival has caused quite a stir, that, I assure you. The chase is on."

Jessica turned, draping the gown over her arm, as she gazed at her Aunt with a stern intensity.

"Well, they can chase all they want. I'm not interested. I'm your companion and that's enough excitement for me. I told you, I'm not ready … and … and I don't think I can ever trust another man again, ever."

As she drew near, her Aunt reached for her hand and pulled her forward to sit beside her upon the bed.

"I know, dear. I know," she patted her hand tenderly. "I don't expect the hurt and fear to dissipate like that," she snapped her fingers. "But, you mustn't build a wall around yourself either. You're smart, stunning, resilient, and have a remarkable future that is awaiting you with adventures, fulfilling accomplishments and wonderful memories, that will last you a lifetime. That life, won't happen, if you aren't willing to suck it up and take risks. Learn from those experiences. Don't let them disable you." She drew Jessica into her arms and hugged her fiercely, then held her at arm's length. "Tomorrow night is about fun, making new acquaintances, and continuing to leave the past where it belongs. Are you willing to do just that?"

Jessica knew that her Aunt was right. Like anything else in life, to move forward, one had to take baby steps. She wasn't about to let her fear of getting hurt, disable her. Not by a long shot. It would be like allowing Richard and Hal to still have a hold over her.

She nodded her acknowledgement slowly. With her Aunt by her side, she could survive her 'coming out' in New York society or any other damn city in the country.

CHAPTER SIX

They took a horse drawn carriage down Fifth Avenue to 82nd Street. It was a gorgeous evening in the city. The crisp Autumn air was refreshing, and the clear, black night sky sparkled with the twinkling of a bazillion stars.

Florence shared short quips of individuals Jessica would most definitely meet that evening. The same circle of socialites always attended such gatherings, and Florence told her, that she would be bored of them quickly. Then, there would be others Jessica needed to avoid extending relations to beyond a simple introduction. Florence promised to steer her away from those most readily.

It was something she never had to familiarize herself with back in Maine. She rarely had the opportunity to attend such gatherings with Richard. Hell, they never had a date night after they were married. Those, she was graced to appear at, were strictly for 'show'. Her gown was always rented. Her jewels were borrowed from her mother-in-law, and she was expected to keep her mouth shut, smile prettily, and basically act like an adornment, and nothing more.

The carriage driver pulled up alongside the curb, where a long red carpet had been stretched out, that led up to the bottom of the Museum's massive staircase. The entrance was flooded in light, as though the opening premier of a movie was being promoted.

Jessica's adrenaline ran hot as blood pumped furiously through her veins, and her excitement climaxed. The "Met", as it was known to all in New York, looked like a white elephant against the evening sky, its many steps leading upwards, as if in homage to a god. She recognized many of the dignitaries entering ahead of them and felt rather privileged to be amongst them.

A distinguished and handsome older gent moved forward to greet them, when they reached the top of the stairs, his face alight with pleasure.

"Florence! What an honor it is to have you grace our presentation. I can't tell you how happy I am that you chose to attend our simple little gala this evening," he bowed, as he brushed the tips of her fingers with his lips.

"Oh, Hayden," her Aunt rebuked playfully with a wave of her free hand. "You don't do simple. We all know that."

He smiled devilishly, tilting his head slightly.

"You know me we well, my beauty." He winked. "But still, my words are true in my happiness to see you," he continued, as he tenderly held her hand between his.

"You are a charming flirt, and you know I adore you." She slipped her hand from his and placed it upon Jessica's arm. "Now, let me introduce you to my niece. Dear, this is Hayden Morrison, Director of the Museum. Hayden, my darling niece, Jessica Rochelle Wilton."

Jessica extended her hand. "It's a pleasure to make your acquaintance, Mr. Morrison."

She liked him immediately for the way he made her Aunt's eyes sparkle. They both seemed to be cut from the same cloth, jarring back and forth playfully. Even a stranger coud tell that they were enamored with each other.

"You are a beauty my dear, but of course, it only compares second to your Aunt's," he gallantly bowed, pressing her fingers to his lips in the same debonair fashion. "I hope you enjoy your evening with us, and it would be an honor, if you pleasured this old man with a dance later this evening. Now, if you'll excuse me ladies, I must greet the rest of my guests."

Jessica bumped her Aunt's side playfully.

"I like your gentleman friend, Aunt Florence, and do believe he has a mad crush on you. I'd set my sights on that one, if I were you. He's a cutie."

"I'm working on it, dear. Men like Hayden love to pursue, and I like playing hard to get. I'll let him catch me eventually."

Her Aunt grabbed two glasses of champagne from a passing waiter, handed one to Jessica, and raised hers in toast to the evening ahead, before taking a slow sip.

It was the 60th Anniversary of the Museum's opening and the guest list transcended any Jessica could have imagined. There were business tycoons, former and present representatives of government, starlets with their leading men from the theatres on

Broadway, New York's socialites, and those from the fashion world.

The champagne flowed, hor'deurves were a plenty, fondues, delectable pastry, and gourmet dip stations were set up everywhere. It was an extravaganza as a twelve-piece big band played continuously for their listening and dancing pleasure hit songs from the past six decades.

Her Aunt introduced her to New York's finest, famed and influential. In turn, they were quite surprised that this had been her first visit to the city. Everyone she talked to professed there was no other city in the world quite like New York.

It got a little old, after the first hour, almost to the point of being lectured to.

"You know dear," former Governor, Lawrence Ives, caught her ear, "I have lived a great deal of my life here, and although I have lived at shorter lengths in others, none is more captivating. It is the nation's most populated, the capital of world finance, business, and communication. It may not be the center of our universe, but it does occupy a central place in the world's lifestyle. Certainly, by any standard, you must agree it affects the lives of nearly every American in one way or the other."

Jessica wanted to look at him like he had two heads, but she responded as demurely as she could muster.

"Governor, I have found that nearly every person in this room shares your sentiments. Everyone, but I, that is," she chuckled lightly, noticing the look of utter surprise, that registered on his face. She raised her point finger quickly to stop him, as his mouth opened in argument. "Please don't get me wrong. A man of your stature and traveling experience, would know this so much more than I. This is my first time visiting, and other than living in Bar Harbor, I have nothing else to compare this city's greatness too." She smiled demurely. "Now, if you'll excuse me."

Jessica quickly exited her retreat, as she exchanged a look of boredom with her Aunt and headed for the nearest exit to catch a breath of fresh air.

The temperature that greeted her was more biting, than when they first arrived. She didn't mind though, as she found it refreshing. Despite the tall buildings, she could tell that the sky was clear, allowing the moon above to alight everything below in its soft glow. She leaned up against one of the huge, white palisades and rested the back of her head against it, closing her eyes and letting the silence embrace her. Slowly, she breathed in deeply and hadn't realized just how thick the air was inside with so much pomp and circumstance strutting about.

Jessica was startled by a voice that came from the other side of the pillar she had been leaning against.

"Really, stuffy inside, isn't it? There's nothing like a little night air to clear one's senses, smog not included, of course."

She didn't know whether she wanted to respond, or just exit quickly.

"My apologies, if I interrupted your quiet time," he continued, making his appearance further known. His features were only slightly notable, as he stood somewhat hidden in the shadow of the same pillar he stood beside.

Jessica swallowed a gasp. What she could see of him, told her he was ruggedly handsome with hair as black as the night. It was like he was holding back, trying not to invade any more of her space than what she might have wanted.

She shook her head, what would probably seem in madness to him, and answered.

"No, no. I, I just didn't expect, didn't see anyone else out here. I'm not use to all that noise and those people. I'm a country girl really, and, oh dear, I'm rambling, aren't I?"

"And, quite a beautiful one, I might add."

She could feel her face begin to flush and prayed that the moon's glow she seemed to be now standing under, did not give away her embarrassment.

"I'm one myself," he titled his head slightly, as he took a step closer. "A country boy, that is. I grew up near a lake with not a tall building in sight. Still can't get use to the hustle and bustle of city life. This one especially."

"Well, that's a first!"

His tone was one of uncertainty as he replied. "The first?"

She chuckled.

"To openly admit your lack of admiration," she replied. "No matter who I spoke to so far this evening expressed nothing but an overabundant love for this city. No other has quite the style," she waved her arm widely. "I guess nowhere are things done in such a grand American way as the Big Apple."

His eyes twinkled, as he moved even closer, and she found herself squinting to see what color they were.

"I know what you mean," he continued. "It's kind of sickening really. Where I come from, the people and the land represent the All-American way."

She couldn't get over the stir he caused inside of her. She loved the smell of his cologne, as it drifted around her on the night air and the deeply-seated dimple she could see at the right corner of his lip. He seemed so familiar somehow, but she couldn't quite place where she could have met him. She wanted to reach out and pull at his arm to draw him out of the shadows, so she could get a better look at him. All she could tell, was that his hair was as black as the tuxedo he wore, which fitted his tall, muscular form nicely. As chiseled as his profile seemed, his charm softened its edges.

She found herself comfortably attracted to him and then it was as if a light bulb went off in her head.

What the hell am I doing? This guy is a total stranger, and I'm goggling over him like a star struck teenager.

Just as quickly, she remembered her conversation earlier with her Aunt. She knew she had to work at not letting Richard's ghost destroy her chance at happiness. She willed herself to relax. Not all men, were like her dead husband. She couldn't let her memory of him, cloud her judgement of others.

"You're Florence's niece, right?"

His question snapped her out of her trance.

"Um … ah … yes," she stammered.

It was like the moon decided to shine much brighter at that moment, as he stepped into its light. Her breath caught in her throat, as she became entranced by the beautiful, blue cobalt of his eyes.

The bewitching attraction was broken, when the sound of someone calling out her name filled the night air.

"Jessie! Jessie, is that you out there dear?" Florence called, as she slowly approached them both. "I was worried and … Bryan! Is that you dear?" She gasped in surprise, as she made her way closer. "Well, I'll be … if, it isn't you!" She exclaimed, as she opened her arms wide to hug him. "You've met my niece again, I see."

He smiled adoringly, as he stepped into her Aunt's embrace.

"Well, Florence, we were just getting …"

"I am such a jerk!" Jessica bellowed. "I should have recognized you, and to think you offered a position on your staff, and I didn't … I so apologize, Senator."

Her look of surprise matched his, as he answered.

"Well, to be quite honest, I didn't know it was you at first either."

"Oh, for Lord's sake you two," Florence blustered, as she pushed the Senator playfully, making him break into laughter. "Let me reacquaint you two. Jessica, you met Bryan rather briefly, which probably explains the confusion, a few weeks ago at a party hosted in his honor. Senator Bryan Gallagher, my niece Jessica, who as you remember, would be a wonderful asset as your Director of Communications."

The Senator reached for her hand and bowed respectfully.

"It's a pleasure Mrs. Wilton, I assure you."

"Not a Mrs., anymore," her Aunt corrected him. "She's quite single, a widow actually. You can call her Jessica, after all, since she may be working for you."

Jessica tried to stifle her laughter and cleared her throat before answering.

"Senator, I'm sure you know my Aunt's bark is worse than her bite. You'll have to excuse her bad manners," she toyed, as she sent her Aunt a sideward glance.

"Well, I'm not the one who forgot they had already been properly introduced. Did I tell you; I've known this young man since his first year in college?"

Jessica shook her head in response, and Florence continued without a beat.

"Hmm. Bad manners, you say. I guess then I'll just leave you two and get back to the reception." She directed her attention to the Senator. "Bryan, you make sure you come by for lunch as soon as you're able, tomorrow, if you can." Before he could reply, she turned about and quickly departed.

"She's like a whirlwind, but still quite the lady." He remarked, as they both watched her Aunt's departure, until she disappeared indoors.

"She most certainly is that, and more." Jessica replied. "I love her dearly."

"Lucky her." He quipped with a smile that made her heart flip inside her chest.

She looked away and shuffled nervously.

"She's the only living relative I have. My mom and dad were taken from me when I was a young child. My grandmother raised me," she added shyly, "and passed a few years ago."

"And your husband's family?"

She was afraid the conversation would go down a path she didn't want to venture. When it did, her head snapped up with surprise, and she hesitated before the words slipped from her lips.

"I ... I buried him nine days ago. His family ... well, they never were very accepting of me."

His look of astonishment wasn't surprising. She knew her Aunt hadn't embellished on Richard's death, the cause, or her history with his family. It wasn't necessary, and quite frankly, she didn't want to go there. She started to feel uncomfortable at the way he looked at her.

"Senator. You're staring," she scolded, and shuffled from one foot to the other.

"I ... my apologies. I can't help myself, or imagine someone like you, not being cherished."

His words were rather unexpected, and she didn't know how quite to respond to them and the way he continued to look at her. It was both unsettling and exhilarating. Still, she knew, if she was going to work with this man, she needed to change the way this conversation was going.

"There's nothing I can do about the past, Senator. I'm here with my Aunt to move on with my life, and I hope your offer still stands for that vacant position in your office. Does it?"

There was no hesitation, as he replied.

"Most definitely. It's yours whenever you want to begin."

"How about first thing Monday morning?"

His smile was warm and welcoming as he answered.

"Monday, it is." He reached for her hand, and she let him. "Let me be the first to welcome you on board. I hope you can learn on the fly, Jessica. Elections are in a month and my opponent is well serving of my seat and a person I respect. I'm not ready to give up my seat on the Senate, just yet. I've got too much work to do.

"That's what I'm hoping for Senator, to be crazy busy, with little time to think of nothing else."

She directed their attention at the sound of the music in the distance and pointed.

"Shall we venture bank indoors?"

Her offered his arm, and she slipped hers though his, clasping his forearm. It felt good walking beside him. She liked his energy and so far, everything about him.

"Do you dance, Senator?"

"You're asking a country boy, if he can dance?"

She laughed at his honesty.

"I've been known to sweep a lady off her feet with a mean waltz though."

Just a few feet from the entrance, someone stepped from the shadows, startling Jessica half out of her wits, making her screech.

"Well, well, well. What do we have here? A tryst in the pale moonlight?"

Jessica didn't know, who the spiteful female was. She could tell from the stiffening of Bryan's arm, that he was put off by the intrusion. The woman's jealously seeped from every pore, and the vehement tone of her voice clearly attested, that she may have some legitimate claim on the man at her side.

Jessica slipped her hand from his arm. The woman looked and smelled of money. The strongest aroma, however, was from the excess of alcohol she apparently had consumed. She was extremely attractive, as her long golden blond tresses swayed from her drunkenness. There was a hardness about her. Her green eyes were not soft, and resonated hatred.

The last thing she wanted, was to get caught up in a scene with a woman obviously out of control.

"I think you misunderstand. If you're the Senator's date, I apologize for keeping him from you."

"Oh, how proper you are. Isn't she darling?" She spewed, as she stumbled forward.

"Angela enough!" The Senator barked.

The woman snickered, ignoring his outburst. "In case Bryan forgot to mention during your little interlude, I am far from just a date. I'm his fiancé, and you are treading where others fear to dare."

The Senator stepped forward, but Jessica reached for his arm and snapped him backward, surprising both he and his fiancé.

"And who may I ask, dares to threaten me?"

"Darling, you wouldn't need to ask, if you traveled in my circle. But since you don't, I'll not waste my breath."

"That's quite enough, Angela." The Senator bellowed. He turned, bowed slightly towards Jessica, and stepped away. He grabbed the woman by her elbow with a vice-like grip, snarling through gritted teeth. "I think you've embarrassed yourself enough for the evening and owe Mrs. Wilton an apology."

Jessica piped in quickly, as she entwined her fingers in front of her.

"No need, Senator. You see she's right. I don't travel in her circle and would never lower my standards to do so."

His fiancé teetered against his side and harrumphed loudly.

"Really? I think not, missy. My riches speak volumes."

Her remark did not discourage Jessica and she simply shrugged.

"That's where you're wrong. There's no price on class. It can't be bought. Even with new money like yours. I would never offer someone like you my time, or my friendship. You see dar-ling, you'll never have the pedigree, style, and grace I was born into."

The Senator chuckled loudly, and it made Jessica smile warmly.

"So, if you'll excuse me," she directed her attention to the Senator, as though the woman at his side never existed. "I'll see you first thing Monday morning."

When she gazed at the woman, still swaying at his side, her mouth was agape from the slap down she had just received.

"Perhaps, we'll meet again under more sobering circumstances."

"Bitch!" The Senator's fiancé screamed, as she departed.

"You know what?" She heard him reply. "Each day I become more aware of your imperfections, and I don't like what I see. I've had just about enough of your antics and outbursts. Grab a cab. I'm done with you."

When Jessica entered through the double French doors, she stepped to the side and shielded herself behind the curtains. She felt bad for the Senator, and somewhat afraid of what his inebriated fiancé might do. She watched and listened, as they drew even closer.

"Bryan, wait!" His fiancé called after him. "Please, darling, wait. Don't leave like this." She caught up to him, pulling at his arm, forcing him to face her. "Stop! Please!"

He huffed heavily. "Angela, you've gone too far, too many times. What we once had, is gone. I can't do this anymore."

"Tread lightly, darling. Daddy wouldn't like the way you're talking to his princess."

Her threat did not fluster him and, he kept on walking, but turned in another direction and took a path that led to the front of the building.

"You'll be sorry, Bryan. Nobody walks out on a Dalton. Do you hear me?" His fiancé screamed at his retreating back.

Jessica scooted away at that moment and headed for the ladies' room. She didn't blame him for just leaving and not coming back inside. She couldn't help but be curious about the woman, and who her father was. Her remark made her wonder, if her father financed his election. Then, as quickly as the thought entered her mind, she dismissed it. She knew it wasn't true. Her Aunt knew him for the man he truly was. He had a good reputation in the Senate. He was the type of man, who wouldn't allow himself to be someone's pawn. He would never bargain his soul for a favor.

A woman like her, wouldn't let this all end without repercussions. Jessica just knew it. Things could get ugly, especially now that she would be joining his staff. She sighed heavily and shook her head in discontent.

"What am I walking into?" She said aloud.

Only time would tell.

CHAPTER SEVEN

Jessica had never slept so soundly, despite
how the evening had turned out. As she rose
from her bed, she noted the time on the digital
clock on her nightstand at nine-fifty-four. She
could not remember the last time she had ever
slept in that late. She hurried with her toiletry
and went in search of her Aunt.

She found Florence outside on the patio,
enjoying a light breakfast poolside.

Florence looked up from reading her
morning paper and smiled warmly, as she
stepped onto the tiled patio.

"Good morning," Jessica offered, sighing
softly as the warmth of the sun's rays greeted
her. "I'm sorry I rose at such a late hour. Did

you sleep well?" She bent to place a tender kiss upon her Aunt's cheek.

"I did. Quite well, dear. Thank you. I'm sorry your evening was ruined by that crass woman."

She took a seat across from her Aunt and reached for the carafe of coffee sitting atop a hot plate.

"I rather enjoyed the exchange to be quite honest," she smiled. "I have to admit; it was good for my ego. I can't remember the last time I stood up to anyone, except Hal, before I left. It was fun."

Cora entered and placed a warm plate of eggs and bacon before her, patted her head tenderly, and exited.

"You know, I really wanted to pop that woman."

"Does my heart good to hear you say that, despite how unladylike it sounds." Her Aunt replied happily. She raised her glass of orange juice in salute. "That's the niece I remember. It's nice to have her back."

"That scared little girl is gone. You, this house, my freedom these past few weeks, are exactly what I needed."

"How about a quick refresher course on state government?"

Jessica shook her head in the negative and swallowed a forkful of eggs.

"I don't think that'll be necessary, Aunt Florence. I couldn't shut down my brain last night and bored myself to sleep researching just that topic and what my responsibilities might be for the position I'll be filling."

"And what did you find?"

She took a sip of coffee, before replying.

"It's going to be challenging, that's for certain. I'm excited though. I look forward to promoting his agenda, leading his media campaign, acting as his press secretary, overseeing his social media sites, helping his constituents and answering his correspondence on his behalf, and whatever else there is I don't know of yet."

They heard the house phone ringing in the distance and shortly thereafter, Clora appeared in the doorway.

"Excuse me, Mrs. Newcombe," she interrupted. "Sen. Gallagher is on the line and requesting to stop by some time this afternoon to meet with you both."

"Poor man. He probably feels as though he needs to apologize for that debacle of a fiancé." Her Aunt offered. "Clora, please tell the Senator to expect to join us for lunch at noon."

"Certainly," Clora nodded and turned to do so.

"He needn't apologize for anything." Jessica shared.

"I agree. Bryan's a gentleman though. I hope he has the good sense of breaking ties with the woman, for his own good, regardless of who her father is."

"Just who is her father?"

Florence waved the question off with a sniff.

"Second generation steel. But, more of a loudmouth thug than anything else. I'm afraid Bryan has been hood-winked by Miss Dalton's beauty, rather than the true she-devil, who dwells beneath that porcelain skin."

Jessica nearly spurted out the coffee she just sipped and laughed. "Say what you really feel, why don't you!"

Florence sent her a miffed look, making her laugh even more.

"I have to admit, I agree. The little time I've spent with him, made me believe he wasn't the type to attach himself to such a woman."

Her Aunt nodded, as she pushed her plate aside and refilled her coffee cup.

"You've chosen well. Bryan Gallagher is an exceptional young man, and you'll make a good team. He just turned thirty and the youngest member, you know, to ever be elected Senator in this state."

"He wasn't always a politician though, right?"

She, too, set her plate aside and settled back to await her Aunt's reply.

"I met Bryan through an acquaintance of your Uncle's. Sen. Walt Markham was Chairman of the Codes Committee, which basically has jurisdiction over all aspects of bills that protect crime victims and punish the criminals. Walt reached out to him after a series of murders plagued the capitol some years back. Bryan was a Lieutenant on the Vice Squad for the City of Albany. They worked on legislation together pertaining to the death penalty. Walt died unexpectedly from a heart attack. Bryan was making quite a name for himself, and the party reached out to him to fill Walt's chair."

"The more I learn of him, the more I like what I hear."

When she noticed the look of approval on her Aunt's face, she waved her point finger at her.

"Don't go reading anymore into that statement. My interest is purely platonic."

Her Aunt smiled knowingly and replied.

"Whatever you say, dear."

She could tell from the look on Florence's face, her Aunt was thinking she had a crush on Bryan. She didn't. She admired him. She found him rather charming and witty, and yes, he was a hunk of burning love, by any woman's standards. The man exuded sexuality for Pete's sake. So much so, she had stirrings of desire she thought would lie dormant forever. Even now, the thought of him left her damp between her thighs.

She shook the idea from her mind. She had to go into this job with the mentality, that

Bryan Gallagher, was her boss. Nothing more. She needed this job to help her start a new chapter in her life, a life of independence and purpose. She needed to prove her worth to herself first and believe it.

"What are you thinking, dear?" Her Aunt's question interrupted her thoughts.

"I just hope this whole thing with Angela settles quietly, that's all. Everything I read on the internet last night, after I got home, tells me he's a very controversial figure."

"You're talking about the death penalty bill?"

Jessica nodded.

"The courts have been battling the constitutionality of that issue for nearly two decades now. The members on both sides of the aisle have voted every year to reinstate it, only to have the bill vetoed by the governor."

"But, haven't a lot of police officer's been killed in the line of duty, and hundreds heartlessly murdered in his state over the past two years. You would think the man, would care enough to want to do more?"

"Yes. I agree. I think his judgment is more personal. He's not listening, to what the people of this state want. He's a devout Catholic and lead by those beliefs."

"But wasn't a family member of his also a victim of such a crime? I could have sworn I read that somewhere."

"A second cousin, dear. Perhaps, for him, it wasn't personal enough. I know Walt is considering not seeking re-election. There's been talk he's looking at something in the private sector. If that happens, the party is seriously considering throwing Bryan's name into the ring."

"Isn't he kind of young and inexperienced to hold a position of such power?"

Her Aunt responded assuredly.

"Quite frankly, no. Young blood is needed. We've had one pompous ass after another using that office as a steppingstone to the White House, Walt MacDonald excluded, of course. He's a good man and has made some monumental changes during his term. We need another man like him, who cares about this State, and its people.

I believe Bryan is just that man. This isn't conjecture, dear. If Bryan's death penalty bill becomes law, it will be a vital ticket to the Governor's mansion. Mark my word. We will see that happen."

The certainty of it all, was a little hard to digest. Just to think the job she would beginning shortly could lead straight to the Governor's office, was a little unsettling, to say the least. She swallowed nervously and reached for her coffee cup, emptying it of its contents.

"Don't let Bryan's good looks fool you, Jessica," her Aunt continued. "Behind that handsome exterior, lies the mind of a felicitous young man. He's attained many honors in his thirty years. He's a Master in self-defense and weaponry, can debate the best of them on the Senate floor, graduated Cum Laude from George Washington University, is bilingual in Spanish, which makes him appealing to a very large minority; and he was awarded a Medal of Valor from his stint with the Marine Corp's Special Operations Command. The young man is one hell of a catch."

They were so engrossed in conversation, they not only lost track of time, but completely unaware that their lunch guest was standing at the threshold between the back parlor and patio.

"Who's one hell of a catch?" Bryan asked, scaring them both out of their wits.

Florence popped to her feet with a started yelp.

"Oh! Dear me. You startled us." She moved to greet him with open arms. "Don't you know it isn't proper to listen in on a lady's conversation," she scolded, as she hugged him tightly, "especially when one is talking about you," she whispered softly in his ear.

"I hope it was good," he whispered back, before placing an affectionate kiss upon her cheek.

"I'm afraid that Jessica and I have been languishing here and so enthralled in catching up, that we clearly let time slip away from us. We truly didn't mean to greet you, still sitting in our loungewear." She apologized, as they made their way back towards Jessica.

He raised his palms to emphasize his point. "Please, don't change on my account. Very seldom do I have the chance to luncheon with two ravishing beauties poolside." He directed his attention Jessica's way and nodded. "Hello Jessica. It's good to see you again."

Jessica smiled warmly and nodded. "Hello, Senator. Good to see you as well."

She couldn't stop the fluttering playing havoc with the pit of her stomach, as she gazed up at him. He was even more striking in the bright light of day. The color of his eyes were magnetizing and she forced herself to look away, as she pointed in the direction of an empty chair.

"Please, have a seat."

"I will," he acknowledged, "if you promise to call me Bryan when we're not out in the public eye."

Like a gentleman, he pulled out the chair Florence had been occupying, but she waved the action off.

"Sit dear."

Clora entered, just as he took a seat to Jessica's right, and nodded his thanks, when she handed him a glass of iced tea.

Florence nodded and continued. "If you two young souls will excuse me, I think I'll go change."

Bryan attempted to rise, but Florence placed her hand upon his shoulder, to stop him.

"Please don't change on my account, Florence."

"Hush now." Florence replied. "I'm getting a little stiff and need to work the kinks out. I'll be back down shortly. Enjoy this beautiful Autumn day," she answered and quickly departed.

His face took on a more serious look, as he gazed at her, and Jessica had an idea where the conversation would turn. She stopped him before he got a change to speak.

"You don't need to say anything, Bryan. It wasn't your fault, that your fiancé had too much to drink last night. Really, it's alright."

He plainly did not agree, as he replied in an adamant tone.

"Well, it's not and we're no longer a couple."

It was no surprise to hear that, after what she witnessed once she left the both of them. She didn't want him to know that though and replied accordingly.

"Oh, Bryan. I truly am sorry to hear that."

He shook his head, as though the decision did not weigh heavily on his mind.

"Don't. I made a grave error in judgement. She wasn't the woman I thought she was."

Jessica scrunched her lips to the side. "I certainly can understand that."

His brows furrowed, as he gazed at her. "How so?"

She waved her hand like a warning signal at a train crossing. "Oh, that's a story for another time, truly. Just know, my feelings were far from hurt. I hope you don't think less of me, when I confide, that I rather enjoyed the exchange."

She could see a chuckle begin to bubble up inside of him, until it escaped.

"You really slapped her down too. I rather enjoyed it myself."

Jessica couldn't contain her own giggles and together they enjoyed the moment of mirth, before attempting to contain themselves.

"Well, with that being said," he paused briefly, "I called upon her this morning to officially break off the engagement and learned that she had left the country on a holiday." He snapped his fingers in the air. "Just like that. Of course, she's avoiding the inevitable but, as far as I'm concerned, it's over."

"All for the better, I suppose."

He nodded slowly. "Yes, all for the better. Jessica, another reason why I wanted to talk to you, is to let you know your official start date won't be until Wednesday."

She tried not to let the disappoint register on her face.

"Oh! You won't be in town, until then?"

He took a hearty sip from his tea, before answering.

"Quite the opposite. I spoke with Marcus Wainright this morning. He's head of the Senate's Journal Clerk's Office. He knows the ins and outs of the legislative process better than the Member's themselves. I thought his instructions would help your transition more smoothly. Marcus will work with you for a few days to explain that process, the breakdown of committees and their realm of responsibility. First thing Wednesday morning at 9 a.m. you'll meet with Senate Personnel to process your paperwork for payroll and insurance coverage. I have a staff meeting set for ten, then you and I will meet for an hour to go over my agenda and will most probably work through lunch, which I'll have ordered in. How does that sound?"

"I, so, can't wait." She replied.

His hearty laughter warmed her insides to a toasty melt down. The dimple to the right of those luscious lips of his was more pronounced than she had remembered.

Please dear Lord, she quietly prayed. *Don't let me disappoint this man. Bless me with the knowledge and intuitiveness to do him proud. Please. Please. Please.*

CHAPTER EIGHT

Sylas Corbat was driven close to the edge of venting his pent-up frustration and wrath for anyone, who got in his way.

The air in the courtroom, one would say, was so tense, you could slice through it with a knife. Sylas knew the bastards sitting in the jury box, would find his brother, Luther, guilty of murder. His brother's lawyer had told him just that morning, that a conviction was inevitable and there would be no chance for acquittal.

Luther was by far meaner and crazier than him. The asshole purposely aimed, shot, and killed those people and that rookie cop, after Luther robbed that grocery store at gunpoint. The god-damned fool never even used a mask to hide his identity, Sylas thought. As much as he hated cops himself, he wouldn't had gone that far.

The judge's pounding of his gavel, aroused Sylas from his musings.

"Mr. Foreman has the jury reached a verdict," Judge Atkins questioned with authority.

"Yes, your Honor, we have," stated a lanky, thin-lipped foreman.

"And what is the decision based on the facts brought forth in this trial against the defendant."

The foreman nervously cleared his throat and brushed the sweat from his brow with a swift swipe of the back of his hand.

"We, the jury, find the defendant, Luther Samuel Corbat, guilty of robbery in the first degree your Honor."

"And on the second count of murder in the first degree?" The judge pursued.

"Guilty, your Honor."

The courtroom disrupted into pandemonium, as the victim's grieving families broke into tears. Those, who sat in witness from the beginning of the trial, until the trial's conclusion, stood and cheered their approval. The Judge's gavel thundered continuously, as it struck home time and again, demanding silence.

"Order! Order! There will be order in this courtroom," the Judge howled. "I will clear this courtroom of everyone, do you hear me?" The Judge's countenance was severe, making the courtroom come to some sense of order. He waited momentarily, until not a whisper could be heard. "Will the defendant please rise?"

Sylas' brother wasn't as accommodating. Stoically, he sat there, staring ahead like a lifeless figure, his eyes leering devilishly.

"Don't play me, Mr. Corbat," Judge Atkins warned. "You can either rise under your own power, or by God, I'll have the officers of this court suspend you from this ceiling." The coldness of his tone and the steely anger reflected in his eyes, was enough to convince anyone of his intention.

Sylas knew his brother's sentencing would not go in his favor. He never played his cards right throughout the entire hearing. His brother had belted one of the guards, breaking the man's nose, he infuriated the Judge with his foul outbursts, and continuously knocked his lawyer for a loop, until he was shackled forcibly. Each act of violence simply added another nail to his coffin. His brother was born mean, with a heart that pumped ice through his veins.

Sylas knew he wasn't an angel either. But, Christ, he wasn't mad like Luther. He liked that people stayed clear of him, and knew most times than not, not to provoke him. He liked it that way.

His brother though, loved conflict, loved to provoke people into giving him a reason to end their lives. He hated school. He hated any kind of authority.

Sy, at least, made it past the ninth grade. He never killed no one ... beat the shit out of many ... but fuck, his brother was crazy.

He watched as his brother finally rose.

"Luther Corbat, you have been found guilty by a jury of your peers. It has been the first time in the history of my court, that such a decision has been made so quickly and accepted by me, as a fair one. In any other circumstance, sir, I would have deemed such a quick decision as unjust. In only honesty, I cannot. The evidence against you is airtight, and due to your outright admission of guilt, I have no other recourse, but to sentence you accordingly. Do you have anything to say to the court, Mr. Corbat, before I pass judgement on you."

Dead silence prevailed over the small room. All whispering and hushed conversations muted. Each person hung on the words they expected the now convicted killer to speak. They had no idea what was to come.

Corbat turned ever-so-slightly and sneered at those sitting behind him. Most gasped and hunkered down lower in their chairs, cowering under his satanic glare. Spittle ran from the corners of lips, as his long, greasy and disheveled locks swayed from his constant nodding, and his eyes glassy reflected his rancor and void of remorse.

Sylas almost expected horns to start breaking through the top of his brother's crown, as he too, looked on.

The Judge broke in. "Apparently, you have nothing to share, Mr. Corbat."

Sylas' brother ignored the judge and turned to glare at the jury. Even though his hands were shackled behind him, as were his ankles, the men and women still flinched in their seats and a few of them gasped in shock.

Luther looked back at the Judge and answered with a hiss to his deep, raspy voice.

"Fuck all you sons of bitches. I killed them and won't grovel to no one. Finish what you got to say, so I can get the fuck out of here!"

The Judge rebuffed his outburst.

"God have mercy on your soul, Luther Corbat. Your evil past has finally caught up with you. Your final act of violence sir will prove the death of you. Under the only remaining portion of this State's death penalty statute, I sentence you to death by lethal injection. I only hope the leaders of our State successfully pass this law soon, so the decent people of this State will get some satisfaction in knowing, that justice is carried out.

In the meantime, sir, you will spend your days on death row. You will never again enjoy the sunshine for any extended length of time, nor will you enjoy the comforts of home, or socializing with decent, honest people. You will serve your term behind bars at Fishkill State Prison, until that time you're put to death. It is my hope that this sentence, brings some sense of comfort to those people you have caused severe harm and sadness too during your lifetime."

With those words spoken, the Judge's gavel struck one last time. "This court is dismissed."

Sylas stood and felt no deep loss for his brother. He pitied the bastard for losing his freedom and getting caught. He knew his brother would go mad locked up. He hated that he'd be used as an example for those pricks to make that bill a law. He hated that their family name would be tied to it as well. People would look at him like he was scum of the earth for his brother's mistake. He turned, after watching his brother being led out of the courtroom. He heard someone call out the name Senator Gallagher and spun about quickly.

His gaze zeroed in on a well-dressed man standing to the back of the room. He saw him in the courtroom during the trial many times and on the news. He was the prick associated with that death bill, always talking himself up to wipe all killers off the face of the Earth.

Yah, that was the guy, he surmised quietly.

He watched as the families gathered around him. He hated men like him, who thought they were all else.

He exited the courtroom and was immediately approached by a well-dressed man he never saw before.

The guy extended his hand in greeting, but Sylas just looked at it like it was a foreign object.

"What the fuck do you want?"

The guy snickered at him and the urge to punch him in the mouth, was almost too hard to ignore. He looked around quickly, noting security and cops in the corridors.

"Your Corbat's brother, aren't you?"

"What business is it of yours?" Sylas shot back.

"There isn't anything you can do for him, I'm afraid. There's a lot I can do for you. Care to listen?"

CHAPTER NINE

Jessica didn't know what was jumping around inside her belly, but it certainly nauseated the heck out of her. She had nervous jitters before, but nothing like this. Her meetings with Marcus had gone exceptionally well over the last couple of days. She was now officially hired, per the Senate Personnel Director, as she exited her office.

The building housing the members of both houses of the New York State Legislature was rather impressive. She was told the walls and floors were constructed of imported white marble that had been shipped in from Vermont and Georgia. As she glided her hands along their cool surface, she knew she was going to love working here.

As she headed toward the elevator, she tried to memorialize this moment in her mind. This was the beginning of yet another chapter in her new life. She blew out a deep breath and depressed the up button for the elevator on the wall in front of her. Almost immediately, the steel doors whooshed open, and she entered, smiling at its occupants, and moved to the side to press the button for the sixth floor.

The conversation going on behind her surprisingly sounded familiar as two gentlemen in their early twenties were discussing the probability of their boss's minimum wage bill making it out of the Labor Committee.

"The Assembly already passed theirs." One gentleman offered. "We've got a majority vote already. All we need now is, for Hinkley to allow a floor vote and we're golden."

"Yah," his companion replied, "when pigs fly."

There was a light chuckle behind her, which made her think it was a sentiment frequently shared around here.

The bell dinged for the sixth floor, and she was the only one exiting the elevator. She took a moment to get her bearings, noticing the sign on the wall to her right showing an arrow for room numbers 600 – 615. She took two deep cleansing breaths to try and calm her still nervous stomach and moved forward. The corridor was a bustle with people in all shapes and sizes. Each legislative office she passed hummed with activity from ringing phones, mixed conversations, laughter, the hum of fax machines, and more.

The door to room 612 was closed. When she reached for the doorknob, it instantly swung inward, startling her. She nearly collided with a rotund gentleman, blocking her way, who was still chatting with a young receptionist, and did not realize Jessica was there.

Jessica's yelp of surprise drew his attention, and he stepped to the side allowing her to enter.

The young receptionist's reaction seemed somewhat perplexing, when she looked her way, and Jessica couldn't imagine why.

"Sorry. Excuse me," Jessica sputtered, as she passed around the man and found herself facing, a taller, stately woman, exiting from another back room. She, too, seemed disconcerted by Jessica's presence, leaving Jessica to wonder whether her presence was not welcomed.

Jessica quickly extended her hand in greeting and introduced herself.

"Good morning. I'm Jessica Wilton and I was …"

The woman let out a breath, as though she was greatly relieved, glanced quickly at the receptionist and then back at Jessica.

Something clearly had just happened between the two women, and Jessica couldn't imagine what the hell it could have been. She didn't have time to question their odd behavior, as the woman quickly stepped forward and wrapped a protective arm about her shoulder.

"Welcome, welcome, Jessica to your home away from home. I'm Claire Martin, Senator Gallagher's, Office Manager." She nodded to the cute receptionist at the front door. "Over there is Missy Sanchez our receptionist and she backs up with secretarial support as well."

Missy nodded happily and offered. "We're excited to have you on board, Mrs. Wilton. Please feel free to ask me anything, okay? Would you like a refreshment?"

Jessica shook her head no and replied.

"Thank you for the kindness, Missy, but I'll pass. I'm sure I'll have questions aplenty, and please, call me Jessica."

Missy smiled and then answered a line that began to ring.

Claire redirected her back through the doorway she had just exited and explained as they continued walking.

"The Senator was called away but will be back in time for your meeting with him at eleven. In the meantime, let me show you around and introduce you to the rest of the staff. You can meet with them all indirectly.

Jessica placed herself in Claire's capable hands, feeling extremely welcomed in her warm and nurturing presence.

She was introduced to Maggie McIntyre, an attractive black woman, who was in her fifth month of pregnancy and acted as Senior Secretary, Zachary Lyons their Legislative Aide, Nicholas Holson, a State University student and Session Intern, and lastly, Connor Taylor, Acting Counsel. The support staff shared one large room, divided into cubicles with tall sound panels, that afforded them some privacy. She and Connor had their own private office, large enough to occupy their desk and chair, a bookcase, and two visitor's chairs. Her office shared a connecting door with Bryan's.

She spent mainly twenty minutes with Claire, Zachary, and Connor, learning the aspects of each of their jobs and how they would interact together.

Connor was a jokester, and she loved his wit and relaxed manner. She wasn't surprised to learn that he and Bryan were lifelong friends, had attended the same University together, and planned on acting as his Counsel throughout his political career. Besides her own duties, she would be working with him closely, writing memos in opposition and support to the legislation he would draft for Bryan, fill in for Bryan and meet with constituent groups and lobbyists, and be Bryan's eyes and ears on the Codes Committee, that he Chaired.

Jessica decided to take a quick break, before Bryan returned to the office and asked Missy where the nearest ladies' room was. The Legislature was in session now, and things would be quiet for a while. When she exited the office, she was surprised to see the hallway empty. She gazed to her right, and all the office doors were closed.

As she turned to the left, she thought it rather strange a man was standing at the end of the corridor, leaning against the wall, and staring back at her. There was something very nefarious about him. His hair was dark brown, long and unkempt about his shoulders, and he wore a tattered and faded Jets baseball cap that rimmed the top of his wide, black eyeglass frames.

He looked at her as though she was someone he was waiting for and pushed himself away from the wall. He pulled down his baseball cap, looked up at the ceiling for some reason and smiled. When he looked her way, his expression was like one of recognition and, maybe, satisfaction.

She looked over her shoulder to see, if perchance, there was someone else behind her, he had recognized. No one was there except for a man, who had just exited a room further down the hallway and went in the opposite direction.

She swallowed nervously, as a warning of fear ran through her. She halted briefly, then questioned, if perhaps, she was just overreacting. He was waiting for someone, that's all, she rationalized in her mind. When she looked back at him, she still didn't feel right. The pressure in her bladder increased, prompting her to move forward, and she did.

She looked directly at him, and the hairs stood at attention at the back of her neck. Goosebumps danced along the skin up and down her right arm.

Something isn't right. Something just isn't right. Her inner voice warned. *What if Hal hired him to find me? Forget the bathroom ... turn around.*

Not even a foot of space separated them, when she made up her mind to retreat down the hallway. It was too late.

The stranger bolted forward and blocked her way, a villainous sneer planted upon his face.

"What changed your mind ... me?"

"I beg your pardon," she shot back, as she tried to side-step around him.

Maybe I can make a mad dash for the bathroom, she rationalized, as she saw the bold black letters that read **LADIES** on the door just a few feet away.

He blocked her way again and she gasped in horror.

"Let me pass please." She glared back at him.

His tiny weasel-like eyes leered back at her through his thick, bifocal glasses.

"You're that Dalton woman. Gallagher's rich fiancé," he spat.

"I am not." She blasted back. She looked at the elevator doors, wishing them to open.

"Don't lie ta me, bitch. I gots your picture right here." He waved a tattered newspaper clipping under her nose.

She stepped back in fear, shaking her head profusely in argument.

"No, you're wrong. My name is Jessica Wilton. I was just hired by the Senator. I can show you my driver's license." She slipped her purse from her shoulder and attempted to open it with fingers, that refused to cooperate.

He clutched her forearm in a vice-like grip, making her squeal painfully.

"Lying bitch," he snarled, increasing the pressure on her arm.

His eyes glazed with anger, as his cheeks flushed and beads of sweat seeped from every pore on his face.

Jessica was horrified at his reaction.

Just in the nick of time, the elevator bell dinged, and the doors glided open, and it was Bryan's face she saw first. It was also obvious to him and the other two male occupants, that something was amiss by the scene taking place in front of them and the look of utter panic on her face.

The madman released her, pushed her hard against the wall, making her slam her head. In a flash, he bolted toward the Exit stairs, and was gone from sight.

She went down hard, as squiggly, white worms danced before her eyes.

Bryan ran forward, catching her, before she hit the floor, while the other two men went in pursuit of the assailant.

"Jessica, shit, are you alright?" He cried out, as he cradled her in his arms, quickly examining her for any obvious signs of injury.

Just then a woman in the office next to them opened the door and looked out.

"My God, I thought I heard something," she blurted and looked down at them both.

"Call the Capitol Police, now!" Bryan demanded.

The woman nodded, turned, and entered her office to do his bidding.

Another office door opened, and staff personnel stepped out. Soon the hallway was amassed with pandemonium.

She looked up at him in a dazed state, as she rubbed at the knot forming at the back of her skull.

"He … he thought I was Angela. Why would he even think that?"

He looked perplexed and his tone conveyed his displeasure.

"There was a posting on line and in the Times Union this morning of her with a new look that at a glance, could pass for you." He replied.

"What? Why would she do that?"

He sent her a look like … really, you need to ask.

"Who would hate you so much to lash out like this?"

He threaded his fingers through his hair and sighed heavily.

"I put a lot of guys behind bars, Jessica, and sponsoring the death penalty bill has placed me on many a shit list, I imagine."

The Capitol Police arrived, as did two EMT's to check her out, pushing a gurney in case she needed to be transported to the nearby emergency room.

Now she knew why Missy and Claire had looked at her strangely, when she first arrived at Bryan's office. Angela and she obviously looked very similar, and that made Jessica want to punch her lights out even more.

What a helluva way to start out her first day at the office. She was pissed. She was embarrassed. She wanted nothing more, than for people to stop fussing over her and scat in all directions.

When she tried to stand, her head whirled as though she had just stepped out of a spin tunnel doing jet speed rotations. Jessica knew she was losing it, as she swayed on legs not strong enough to assist her and her knees buckled under her. The back of her head throbbed painfully and all she wanted to do was close her eyes and fall asleep.

She looked at the EMT at her side and the words she tried to speak were difficult as she muttered before she slumped against him, "I … no … not good …"

Bryan could tell from the look on Florence's face, that she was not happy, as she made her way into Jessica's room. He took the liberty of ordering a private room for her, so she could be watched more closely.

"What the hell happened to my niece?" She blared, as she moved to Jessica's bedside.

She petted her forehead tenderly and leaned in to place a soft kiss upon her cheek.

"Aunt Florence, I'm fine. Just a large bump on my head. They want to keep me overnight for observation, that's all."

"Don't make light of this, dear. Someone tried to accost you, did they not?"

"Well –"

"Well, nothing," her Aunt barked, directing her attention back to Bryan. "I'm waiting, young man."

Bryan took Florence's temperament in stride. He would be reacting the same way, if he was in her shoes. The one thing he wasn't doing, was taking this situation lightly. He would find the bastard, who did this, and quickly. There was no love lost between him and Angela, but to use someone close to him, as some act of revenge, didn't sit right with him.

"This whole thing was related to me, for some reason. The perpetrator mistook Jessica for Angela, and I believe, attempted to kidnap her."

"I saw the photo of her in the Times and thought so myself. This is her way of getting back at you for the other evening, I suppose."

Bryan nodded and replied, "It could be, in some warped way."

"Or think of it as a compliment to me," Jessica chided in with a snicker, "You know," she shrugged, "to emulate herself in my image." She smiled tritely.

Florence made a face that had Jessica chuckling.

"I don't find that humorous, dear. Imbalanced and unstable, maybe. What if Angela is in cahoots with this madman? Have you thought about that?"

"It's crossed my mind, and certainly something being considered. I've instructed the Capitol Police to pull the feeds from the security cameras and run a face recognition against state and federal records to see, if we can come up with a match and go from there. Plus, we're trying to track down Angela's whereabouts. She's incognito right now and all I'm getting from her family is she's abroad somewhere on the French Riviera."

Florence harrumphed. "Highly unlikely. I still say her fingerprint is all over this."

Jessica held her head briefly and sighed.

"I just can't believe she would do something like this. I mean think about it. She's a socialite. She loves the attention, being in the limelight, having the freedom to come and go as she pleases. Do you really think she would jeopardize all of that, because she thought we had a tryst?"

Florence raised her eyes to the ceiling and scoffed.

"She's vain enough, culpable enough, and stupid enough to hire someone to do her dirty work <u>and</u> think she can get away with it."

Jessica scrunched her lips to the side and replied in a deflated tone.

"I suppose you're right."

Bryan reached for her hand and held it tenderly between his own. What he really, wanted, was to crawl in beside her, and hold her in his arms. He never felt that strongly for someone he briefly knew. But, there was something about this woman that made him want to protect and take care of her. Something had happened to her, something so traumatic, it left a deep scar and created a barrier, an impenetrable one. He wanted nothing more, than to be the one to break down that wall and have her view him in a different light.

This whole incident didn't help. He could see the fear in her eyes, and it bothered him deeply, that he was the cause. He was determined to get to the bottom of this, one way or the other, and the minute he left this hospital, he vowed to himself, he would do just that.

CHAPTER TEN

"Levitt, where the hell is Corbat?" Peter Tallon, owner of Howe Caverns, bellowed loudly.

His place was a public attraction and elaborate series of caverns two-hundred feet underground with a river, lake, and wondrous rock formations.

"Gee, boss, I think he's in the bridal chamber checking on the lights," answered Morris Levitt, an especially nervous and lanky co-worker.

Peter Tallon was hard core all the way and didn't care for any horseplay, notably so, if it meant he was losing money, or looking the fool. He wasn't very happy with Sylas Corbat right now.

"Get your boney ass down there and tell that son of a bitch I want him up here. Now, move it!" He roared, as he stuffed a half-chewed stogy between his yellowed teeth.

In May of 1842, a farmer by the name of Lester Howe noticed his cattle always kept to the far corner of his property during the heat of the summer months. When he went to investigate why and cut away an overgrowth of bushes, he noticed a small entrance from where a blowout of cool, moist air drafted outward.

Little did he know then that it would be noted as the largest cavern in New York State and the means of making him quite a fortune. Now, the caverns had been closed, under the new ownership of Peter Tallon.

The bridal chamber was a pretty, extraordinary crypt, a grotto of luminous rock shaped in the form of a heart, where many romantics loved to exchange their marriage vows.

Sylas was restringing a new formation of intricate lighting down there, when his coworker approached.

"I don't know what the hell you've done to piss off Tallon, Sy, but you better move your ass and quick. He wants you topside, and now." He flustered, as his brow dotted with nervous sweat.

"Jerk off, Levitt! I've got this system to install before dark. I ain't got time!" Sylas remarked irritably.

"Come on, man. I ain't shitting you! Tallon sent me after ya, and if you know what's good for you, you'll burn the soles off your shoes and get up there quick." He retaliated in defense, as he climbed the scaling ladder that hugged the walls of the chamber.

Sylas threw his screwdriver across the chamber, chipping a section of rose-tinted rock from its bed in the process, missing the lanky kid by an inch.

"What the frig is eating at his craw? He wanted this god-damned job finished before dark!" He wailed, scaring Morris to the point, he cowered out of his reach.

Morris watched him from a distance, as his beer belly raked atop each rung of the ladder, while he descended to the floor level below. The man gave him the creeps. The guy rarely smiled or joked for the pleasure of it. A hundred feet below the surface was the perfect place for a man like him.

Sylas had it with Tallon pulling his chain, he argued silently, as he made his way to the entrance. If he had another rush job for him to finish before dark, he'd tell him to go screw. Tallon wouldn't want to provoke him, if he knew what was good for him. He needed him. He knew these caves like the back of his hand. He worked them for eighteen years. He could get him ready for business within a week, if he wanted.

He had Tallon where he wanted him and sneered from the pleasure of knowing it. He loved controlling people.

His shirt was soaking wet with perspiration by the time he reached top. Grotesque masses of curly chest hair glistened, as it peeked from the neckline of his shirt and between the button spaces, that pulled apart from his bulging stomach.

"Took you long enough to get here," Tallon chastised, as he pulled his cigar from his mouth

"You got something to say, get on with it. I've got work to finish in the hole, which you wanted done by dark, remember?" Sylas retorted, as his insides worked into a knot.

Tallon looked at the fists clenching tightly at Corbat's side. He knew the man was pissed already.

"You won't need to finish. Someone else will do it."

"Why the hell not? You think they can do it better than me?"

Tallon shook his head and readied himself for the explosion he knew was inevitable.

"It's a risk I'm gonna have to take. You're out of here, Corbat. Pack your belongings and go." He pulled an envelope containing a check from his pocket and held it out in front of him. "Here's a severance check for your troubles. I can't keep you on anymore."

"You what? Just like that? Why the hell not? You got no call to let me go," he stepped forward threatening. "I'm the best you got here."

Tallon raised his arms in protest.

"Look. You've been down in the hole almost eighteen hours now, and I don't think you know, so I'll tell you."

"Tell we what?"

Corbat was furious and reached for him. He didn't take to being fucked over and this prick was going to feel his fist breaking the bones in his face.

Tallon was prepared. He expected this kind of reaction and drew a pistol from his side vest pocket.

"Back off, dickhead, before I blow your brains out. I'm gonna give you an explanation, because I owe you that much," Tallon continued, as he threw the envelope at him. "Your brother was being transported to Dannemora early this morning. They still don't know how the prick pulled it off, but he got away and killed the two cops transporting him. He hijacked a car and was intercepted by a Trooper, who was the Governor's son. Gunfire was exchanged. The trooper is fighting for his life. He managed to put a few into your brother.

I got a business to run here. I don't need any of this shit, or the attention it'll draw. If people find out you work here, they'll wonder what kind of place I'm running. I need you out of here, cause I certainly don't need any frigging reporters buzzing around either and creating bad press before I open."

"You, bastard. You'll be sorry for this, Tallon. Damn sorry."

He leaned over and picked up the envelope from the ground, sneered at Tallon one last time, and spun about in retreat. He would pay, Sylas vowed. He would pay dearly for firing him. He had plans for those caverns, and getting on the wrong side of him, Tallon would regret. He had no control over his brother, and it wasn't fair he was being fired, because of him. His brother was a sick fuck, but he knew how to get even. Eighteen years was a long time to devote to a job.

Even though the pay wasn't glamorous, he loved what he did, loved working beneath ground, not having to deal with people, alone with the dark and the silence. He knew every stretch of the caverns … the entire mile and a half. He knew of places that hadn't been opened to the public, that the owners didn't want to invest more money in.

He had broken into one of those chambers and had plans for it. Didn't matter now, that he got fired. He didn't need keys. He knew how to get in without them. He was the only one who knew. Nothing would keep him away. Nothing.

CHAPTER ELEVEN

Bryan exited his car and walked the short distance where he generally met up with his snitch down at the Port of Albany. He never lost touch with him once he took office. You never stopped being a cop. It was ingrained in you like your DNA. There were a lot of skills he had developed during his decade with Albany P.D., that came in handy at the Capitol.

He needed to talk to Dante and have him check around and see, if he heard any talk on the streets about the attack on Jessica. He knew, whoever this guy was, had it out for him. This was a vendetta, and what he did to Jessica, was simply a warning.

After reviewing the security tapes from the cameras, Bryan's conclusion wasn't wrong. The bastard had the balls to look straight into the camera and smile. He was sending a clear message to him. He felt it in his gut. The one thing about most criminals, they liked to boast. Bryan hoped this bastard got hard talking about what he got away with.

The assailant was smart too. He knew to pull his baseball cap down just enough to hide his features. The facial recognition he had called for came up short. A tough break for them, but he wasn't about to give up. Now, it was time to hit the streets and branch out. He wished he could have gotten to this sooner, but his calendar was crazy, now that Session was in full swing. Shortly, the Legislature would be breaking for the holidays and there were a lot of bills still sitting in his Codes Committee that needed to be addressed.

Investigators from the State Police had been called in to take the case over from the Capitol Police. It was understandable, but Bryan was comfortable working with his former buddies at the P.D.

When he was a detective, they worked tirelessly and proficiently, cracking homicide cases and cleaning up the streets. His team had worked with the Justice Department to create a cease fire with the area gangs. The city streets were being ripped by gun violence. A week never went by without someone being gunned down in broad daylight.

Dante was a leader of one of the most violent gangs in Albany, known as the Jungle Gangsters'. After three members of his own family were gunned down, including his young wife and five-month-old daughter, he agreed to help stem the bloodshed, after Bryan reached out to him.

Their rapport was still strong, six years strong at working together and slowly making changes. Bryan had gained a valuable insight into the culture of violence that plagued his city. Kids as young as ten and eleven, were being sworn in under the mentality they needed to, in order, to survive on the streets.

Bryan's eyes adjusted to the darkness, and he recognized the landmark silhouettes around the port, where he and Dante always met. He pursed his lips and whistled, a sound, that only Dante would be familiar with. Within a matter of seconds, Dante returned the call and stepped out of the shadows. He spoke in Spanish, since he knew that Bryan would understand.

"Hey, hombre. It has been too long?"

Bryan reached him in three steps, extended his hand, and pulled him in, as they bumped shoulders in greeting.

"I hear you have a new wife and twins. You are well?"

"I have been blessed, yes. One day we will move from here. But, my friend, you are here for a reason, yes?"

Bryan smiled and cut to the chase, replying.

"There was an incident a few weeks ago at my office. Have you heard anything about it by now?"

The gang leader gave one shake of his head and shrugged nonchalantly.

"If you do –"

Dante interrupted. "I will let you know."

Bryan had no reason to think, that Dante would withhold any information from him. Their relationship was built on years of trust, of borderline working the system, so that lives could be saved, so that the inner-city kids had a better chance of growing up to be successful and productive adults.

They shook hands and departed without exchanging any other words.

Once Bryan entered his car, he checked the time on his cell. It seemed much later than 6 p.m. Once the clocks were changed, it got darker earlier and soon it would be Thanksgiving. He thought of Jessica and a craving to hear her voice washed over him. He called her line at the office and the connection was immediate, as she answered right away.

"Hello, this is Jessica."

"Hey, it's Bryan."

"Did you just remember, that you forgot your notes for your meeting with Sen. Talbot tomorrow?"

Bryan smiled inwardly. She had only been working with him a few weeks now, and she knew him well. He had totally forgotten about his notes but used it as an opportunity to draw her out.

"As a matter of fact, yes. You wrapping up there?"

"I am. I can stay though if you're coming back."

"Do me a favor, grab my notes and meet me for dinner. I'm starved, I know you barely took a break today, and we can go over them together?"

There was only a short pause, before she replied.

"Where do you want to meet up?"

"I'm just a few blocks away. I'll meet you out front and drive you back to your car later."

"Okay, I'll wait for you downstairs."

She had just hung up her phone, when her line rang again, and she chuckled, figuring it was Bryan.

"Did you forget something else?" She chuckled.

"I haven't forgotten you for one single moment. Have you forgotten me?"

The sound of his voice made her body shudder and that feeling of needing to throw up tickled the back of her throat. She knew at one point in time, that she might hear from Richard's father again. She hadn't expected it to be this soon. Her voice was venomous as she replied.

"How did you find me?"

"When you have money, my dear, anything is possible. You didn't answer me."

"It doesn't warrant an answer and this conversation is over, Hal."

"Oh, come on! Have dinner with your old father-in-law? Let bygones be bygones, as they say."

"I want nothing to do with you, ever again. Do you hear me? And, if you continue to harass me, I'll see that charges are brought up against you."

She slammed the phone down in his ear and stared harshly at it, visualizing his face and then closed her lids tightly.

What now? Whatever is he up too?

A thousand other questions filled her mind, and she hated the fact he might prove a bone of contention. He just couldn't leave her alone. There were dozens of women he could have right there in Maine, who would jump at a chance of being his paramour. Why couldn't he just leave her alone? She checked her watch, and knew she had to hurry. Bryan would be pulling up downstairs shortly.

She decided not to say anything to him. She wouldn't be surprised, if Hal just called to goat her. He had a sick sense of humor like that. She wasn't about to let him ruin her evening with Bryan.

Jessica had pretty much gotten used to Bryan's crazy hours. She didn't mind it at all. Her days flew by quickly, and for the first time in her life, she felt fulfilled, useful, and pretty, damn awesome about her new life. There were so many facets of her job she loved. Having the opportunity to join Bryan in the Senate Chambers, when he needed her, being recognized, and respected for the position she held on his staff, meeting constituents that adored him, and attending important meetings as his liaison were pretty much a part of her world every day, but still cool and exciting. Life was good, finally, and she wouldn't have it any other way.

She had put the incident outside his office, out of her mind. Security was beefed up, she was escorted to her car every night, and she knew that the State Police were actively looking for the man, who tried to accost her. If she dwelled on it, it would only reopen old wounds she'd sooner forget. Jessica didn't want fear, any kind of fear, to have a hold over her life ever again.

She hadn't told Bryan yet, that she had purchased a small snub-nose revolver to keep in her shoulder bag. She also took lessons at a nearby gun range to learn how to aim and fire it accurately. It wasn't against the law for her to do so, just as long, as she kept it concealed. With that madman still running around, she wasn't going to take any more chances.

She also took self-defense classes on Saturday mornings at the YWCA. It was something she should have done a long time ago. Jessica knew her best protection was being aware and knowing how to fend off an attacker.

Bryan tooted, when he pulled up in front of the Legislative Office Building, and Jessica exited immediately.

He was quite the gentleman, as he stepped from his car and walked around to open the passenger door for her and waited, until she was comfortably seated inside.

He smiled warmly upon entering and buckled his seatbelt.

"How does Angelo's Prime sound?"

"A little pricey, don't you think?"

"Hey, you deserve it. You've been a lifesaver."

Jessica was tickled that he thought so. She needed to hear that, considering, her last phone conversation. If anyone could make her forget, Bryan could. It wasn't easy working so closely beside him every day. She wouldn't change it for anything in the world. Her attraction for him was stronger than ever. She tried to keep her feelings at bay and not let her expressions give an impression of what was raging inside of her. As much as she feared involvement with another man, every day with him, working beside him, seeing him in action, even at his worse, was a true testament to just how wonderful he was.

"Not just me, Bryan. You staff is truly commendable. I can't express enough how impressed I am by their working acumen and dedication to you."

"Oh, I agree and show my appreciation individually whenever I can. Tonight, it's your turn."

She nodded respectfully and smiled.

"Well, thank you."

The look in his eyes, told her there was something more and she quickly looked away. She didn't want to believe it was anything more … well, she did, but she knew she shouldn't. She dug in her briefcase for his notes and pulled them out quickly.

"I looked over these briefly and they're a … a …"

"Scattered mess," he answered for her, chuckling.

She returned his smile and giggled softly.

"Well, I wouldn't go quite that far, but close."

"I agree. My thoughts were all over the place. Sen. Talbot is a man I need in my corner. If I can get his support on the DP bill (death penalty), then more will follow his lead."

"Look, to get a handle on the serious murder rate in this state, this bill needs to be passed, Bryan," She answered. "You know, and I know, that it's not going to solve the problem, but it sure as hell will make criminals think about killing someone and give the system a chance to right itself in time."

He pondered her words thoughtfully, as he pulled into the restaurant's parking lot and up to the valet parking area. Two cars were ahead of them, as he turned to answer.

"You make a good point. There are key questions I know will come up like does capital punishment deter crime? Will innocent people be executed? Am I pursuing it to further my career? Will the statutes unfairly target minorities?"

"And probably," she interrupted, "what the financial impact on the state will be?"

"Yes, that too," he agreed. "If we can get through these over dinner, then I think we have a good chance at winning Talbot over."

Two valets quickly appeared to open each of their doors, they exited, and together entered the establishment.

Angelo's was one of the city's most upscale steakhouses. It was extremely popular with the members and their staff, because of its proximity to the Capitol. It had the class and flair of the dinner clubs back during the Roaring 20's, and the modern sophistication of a five-star restaurant. It took them nearly fifteen minutes to make their way to the table they were being escorted to, as they were stopped by acquaintances, colleagues, and other government officials.

Jessica was surprised they got a table so quickly, as her chair was gallantly pulled out by Bryan for her to be seated.

"Aren't we the lucky ones to get seated so fast," she stated, as their hostess handed them each a menu.

"I called and requested a table after we spoke," he admitted, and playfully raised his eyebrows at her.

Jessica shook her head in amazement. He was quite the man, this Senator of hers.

Their waiter approached, introducing himself, and began to recite the specials for the evening. They listened intently and Bryan immediately ordered a bottle of Sauvignon for them to share.

Jessica released a deep sigh of contentment, as she sat back in her chair, slipped the heels from her feet, and rubbed the soles of her feet against the carpeted floor.

"It has been quite a week. Where does the time go?"

"You're playing in the big leagues now. There is no such thing as time where we work. Business happens no matter the hour."

"I heard the farther we get into Session, the longer the hours become. Is it true, that you're sometimes in chambers, until two ... three ... four o'clock in the morning?"

"Um hmm," he uttered. "The staff of the members will wear their slippers, bring in their pillows, snacks, and yes, we even allow spirits within reason. It's tradition and kicks in around budget time, and doesn't stop, until we break for summer."

"Nothing quite like it, I suppose."

"What I like to do is give the staff comp time. Because everyone is salaried, there's no overtime pay. So, Claire keeps count of everyone's o.t. past 5 p.m., and then the staff is awarded that time off with salary, during the summer. The only one, who doesn't, are the interns, but I compensate them with a nice cash gift card on their last day."

"You're a very just and decent man, Bryan Gallagher." She offered.

He bowed slightly.

"It's the way my parents raised me. They get all the credit."

She raised her point finger to emphasize her remark.

"That may be true, but one can be gravely influenced by outside sources. You've chosen not to be."

The waiter arrived with their bottle of wine. He poured a mouthful for Bryan to test. When

Bryan did so, and nodded his pleasure, their glasses were filled, and the waiter departed.

Bryan raised his glass to toast, and Jessica followed suit.

"Here's to the women, who mold us, to the women, who keep us in line, and the women, who dare to love us."

His message was loud and clear, as the look in his eyes, reflected what he wanted her to feel, to know, and act upon. She clinked her glass softly against his. Her eyes never wavered from his and her right brow lifted ever-so-slightly in acknowledgment, and he did the same.

Jessica was glad the waiter had chosen to return at that precise moment to take their orders. The interruption helped to quell the awkwardness she felt. It was only moments later they fell back into that same rhythm of ease always existent between them.

Bryan had a wonderful sense of humor and was quick to come back with a witty remark, that always left her chuckling. To her, nothing was sexier and more attractive, than a man, who could make a woman laugh.

Throughout dinner, they addressed Bryan's questions and concerns. She took thorough notes, because she knew she would have to prepare speeches for him in the very near future and answer questions herself, reporters would ask.

When their dishes were whisked away, they passed on coffee and dessert, and the last glass of wine was poured, Bryan took her by surprise with a personal question of his own.

"Are you happy with me?"

She knew a dumb-founded look passed over her face like a shade being drawn.

Umm. Umm. Kept repeating in her head like a broken record. She didn't know, how quite to answer. *Did he mean personally*? Her brows furrowed deeply.

"You know, with the office," he prompted, "the staff, your position, us working together," he emphasized, as he waved his hand back and forth between them.

Her mouth opened and closed like a guppy, and she replied, feeling foolish, as she rolled the stem of her wine glass between her point and thumb fingers.

"Yes! Yes, of course. I couldn't be happier."

He reached out and brushed the tip of his fingers over the top of her hand just then and the reaction was totally unexpected. It was like an electrical surge coursed through her veins, shooting up her arm, and sparked the hairs on the back of her head.

The sincere look of fondness in his eyes made her want to sigh deeply, but she contained herself.

"I need to say something here, but I … I don't want you to feel … well –"

She wanted to hear it … whatever it was, and she prompted him along.

"Go ahead."

"Jessica, the first time I met you at my fundraiser with your Aunt, I damn near felt like I was zapped by a Taser."

She couldn't contain herself and chuckled, "In a good way, I hope."

He took her hand in his, and his thumb glided softly over her knuckles.

"Yes," he smiled, and his dimple deepened, making her heart lurch.

God! Those eyes of his. I could stay lost in them forever! She avowed silently.

"Jessica," he continued, "I don't know, if what I'm feeling is mutual, but if it is, I sure would love to pursue it."

When she opened her mouth to speak, he raised his other hand to stop her.

"Hear me out first, please."

She nodded slowly in the affirmative and let him.

"I know you've been hurt deeply, terribly, that … your husband was a brutal man."

She knew her face registered shock. She couldn't hide it.

"The circles we travel in, everyone knew of the Wilton's reputations … all of them. I'm not like him, and never would be." He placed his palm over his heart. "By the soul of my mom, my grandmothers and female ancestors before them, I am not that man. I know the scars left by him, run deep. I can and would be patient. I would love to spend time with you on a more personal level … see a movie, have more dinner dates, go hiking, or biking and dancing, take cooking classes together, whatever you wish. How do you feel about that?"

Holy smokes! He wants to date me. The boss wants us to be a couple ... a State Senator ... me?

She gulped down the remaining contents in her glass. Her head was spinning with a lot of arguments in one respect, and in another, she wanted to jump on the tabletop and do an Irish gig. She gazed back at him and said the next thing that came to mind.

"Is that allowed?"

A hearty laugh escaped his lips, before he replied.

"Well, there's nothing in the Senate rule books, that I know of." He jibed. "You're a widow. I'm unattached. We're two consenting adults. I'm speaking of a platonic relationship right now for the time being, until we see, if something can grow from what I feel is building between us."

How could she say no to this man? Why would she want to? Every moment, every day she has spent in his presence, were by far, some of the best, ever in her entire life.

Besides, Florence simply adored him, and if her Aunt held him in the highest regard, she need not have to worry further. The question was, was she ready to open her heart and take a chance on love again? As she looked deeply into those cobalt blue eyes of his and felt the caress of his hand on hers, she was lost, and smitten, and mesmerized.

"I won't hurt you, Jessica. On my honor, I will treat you with the greatest respect and kindness."

She sighed deeply this time. Her head was agreeing with her heart and blasting out the words, "SAY YES, YOU DAMN FOOL!"

I'm trusting you, Lord. She silently prayed. *Trusting, that this man you brought into my life, is, for those reasons I've only wished and hoped for.*

"Cooking classes, hah?" She couldn't help, but tease.

"That and more," he replied.

"Then, I would love nothing more."

His smile told her, that he was ecstatic, and his joy filled her with happiness.

She did not doubt the decision she had just made. She could see a life with this man, beyond the politics, beside him, supporting him, working with him on future campaigns, if that was to be. Her future looked bright, whether at his side as a member of his executive staff, or known as the man, who stole her heart. Whatever position she was to hold in his life, she would welcome the possibilities.

The waiter approached their table, when Bryan turned to signal him for the check.

"It's been a long day and we've got an early start tomorrow," he offered. "I can either take you back to the garage for your car, or drop you home and pick you up in the morning. Which do you prefer?"

"Do you think my car will be safe, after what happened?"

"You're in an executive staff section that's patrolled by the Capitol Police on a regular basis. It'll be fine, and I kind of like the idea of driving my date home."

"So, you had this planned, as an official date all along?"

"Am I bad?" He pouted playfully.

She smiled in return. He was a man a woman simply could never say no too, but she'd keep him guessing anyways.

"Shall we go then?" She answered, rising from her chair.

He popped up quickly, chuckling lightly, as he moved around and pulled her chair back out of her way.

She loved the feel of his palm against her back, as he led her toward the entrance. She couldn't help, but wonder, if he would attempt kissing her goodnight. One thing was certain though ... she wouldn't shy away ... if he did.

The drive home to her Aunt's house was a pleasant one, filled with more personal conversation. He prodded a little about her parents, her relationship with her Aunt, what she liked to do, and where she saw herself in the next five years.

She didn't hold back answering and was quite pleased, when he shared her sentiments. He wasn't guarded about wanting a family ... four kids exactly ... two boys and two girls, if luck had it. She loved that he had a deep-seeded passion for making the streets safe, giving the less advantaged a better chance to improve their lifestyles, and get the homeless into workable shelters and create opportunities, where they could be self-sufficient once again.

Her Aunt's house was dark, except for the sconces on each side of the front door, and the security lights that went on as they entered the long driveway.

He reached for her hand to help her exit his car and did not let go of it, as he escorted her to the front door. She loved the feel of her fingers entwined with his and hated breaking the connection, when she searched in her purse for her keys.

The tone of his voice was warm and seductive, as he asked, "May I kiss you, goodnight."

Her voice was of no use, as the words lodged in her throat. All she could manage was a simple nod.

It was the only acknowledgment he needed, as he reached up to take hold of her face tenderly. He lowered his mouth slowly, as if to torture her, making her gasp ever-so-slightly. It was worth the wait though, as the warmth of his lips covered hers.

His kiss was firm, and slow, and consuming. This was a man, who knew how to kiss a woman and forever bond her to him. The way he held her face in his hands, made her feel like a cherished, prized, porcelain collection.

She stepped closer, bodies touching, feeling his heat pass through her, and she was spellbound.

The moments passed, and when he pulled his lips from hers, she had all to do to not whimper her disappointment. She held strong, took a step back, managed to find the keyhole, and whispered her goodnight.

"Seven a.m., beautiful," he called out, as she entered the lobby of her Aunt's home. "I'll pick you up with a light latte, and no sugar to go."

CHAPTER TWELVE

Jessica just finished a conversation, when her intercom buzzed, and she answered it immediately.

"Yes, Senator."

"Jessica, I need you and Connor in here quick!"

"Right away," she replied, curious as to the urgency in his voice. She quickly popped from her seat and scurried to Connor's office. The door was open, and she poked her head around the corner. "Something's up. Bryan wants us in his office pronto!"

They entered via the connecting door just in time to see a news break flashing across the flat screen, hanging over the credenza in Bryan's spacious office.

"Good afternoon Channel 10 viewers. This is Bob Killian, bringing you a special report from field reporter, Yancy Hamilton, now live at the Governor's Mansion. Yancy, can you tell us what is happening?"

"Bob, we've just received word, that Governor Michaelson's second youngest son, Warren, has been fatally wounded during a conflict with convicted killer, Luther Corbat, who escaped transport a short while ago to the state penitentiary at Dannemora.

From reports coming in with officers on the scene, Trooper Michaelson, was on patrol in the Indian Lake Region South of Route 30, when a call was dispatched requesting his assistance in the interception of a late model grey, Chevy sedan believed to be driven by Corbat.

For those of you, who may not remember, Luther Corbat, was convicted of murder and robbery and sentenced to serve his time on death row. Corbat apparently ran a check-point set up by Trooper Michaelson outside the town of Newcomb. Corbat bolted from the stolen car, firing. The exchange was said to last only a matter of minutes before back-up from other local authorities arrived on the scene.

Trooper Michaelson was shot, but managed to incapacitate Corbat, before he went down." Hamilton provided.

"Yancy", Killian continued questioning, "have we had any word on where they have taken both? Is the Governor's son expected to survive?"

Yancy replied. "Bob, both were transported by State Police helicopter to Gloversville Medical Center. Corbat has received medical attention and will be transferred to the infirmary at Dannemora under heavy guard within the hour. The Governor's son, however, was not as fortunate and undergoing surgery in a fight for his life for removal of a bullet lodged just below his heart."

"Has the Governor left for Gloversville?"

"He is, Bob, along with the First Lady. As you can see," she turned and pointed skyward, "a state police helicopter is just now taking off."

"Thank you, Yancy." The camera directed back to the anchor. "Well, you've heard it first here and, if you're just tuning in, Governor Richard Michaelson's 21-year-old son, State Trooper Warren Michaelson, has been shot by convicted killer and escapee, Luther Corbat, just minutes ago. Corbat, who was in turn shot by Trooper Michaelson, is now in custody and awaiting transference within the hour to Dannemora State Penitentiary.

We will have a special report following the six o'clock news this evening, and hopefully, will have an update, as to the condition of the Governor's son, who is now undergoing surgery in a battle to save his life. Our prayers are with him and his family. We will now return you to the regularly scheduled program still in progress. This is Bill Killian reporting with Channel 10 news."

Connor was the first to speak, breaking the moment of silence in the room, as Bryan switched off the tv.

"Senator, this, you know, will tip the scales in your favor. Callous as it may sound, but it's true."

Jessica concurred. "He's right. Michaelson was always borderline. Now, that this has hit so close to home, the probability of him signing is stronger than ever. This may just prove the deciding factor."

The look on his face was grave. Jessica knew he didn't want to win this way, but fate had a way sometimes, trumping the cards in one's favor.

He vocalized her thoughts.

"I know. I … I just don't want anyone to think I'm riding on this personal tragedy for my own gain." Warily, he rubbed at his forehead, rose and paced back and forth before them.

"Look, Bryan," Connor spoke in a concerned tone, "let us do the worrying. You just debate the issue like you've been doing all along. The people will know you're just doing the job you were elected to do. It's not anything they haven't heard before.

This issue's been debated for years. Don't forget, three-quarters of the people in this state already wanted it. What happened just now," he pointed, "will sway damn near the rest of them."

Jessica stepped forward, reaching for his forearm tenderly, smiling weakly.

"Connor is right, Bryan. What's important, is not sitting back in the corner. It's time to fight harder and continue the pressure, until it passes both houses. Now that it's out of committee, there's no stopping it."

Bryan threw his hands into the air in supplication.

"I know. I know."

Jessica and Connor exchanged worried looks. Nothing else was said, while their boss continued to pace before them for a matter of seconds, before returning to his chair and sitting down.

When he looked up and saw them both standing there he remarked, "Well, what are you waiting for? Let's get this done. Jessica, dig out the files.

We need for a conference with the membership following the close of session in the East Lobby meeting room. Connor, get everyone on the phones. Advise the member's offices I've got an announcement to make they need to hear, or they may find themselves with egg on their faces, once I go public, if they don't show. Say nothing else."

"Yes, boss!" They chimed in unison, exiting his office shoulder-to-shoulder, discussing his strategy.

CHAPTER THIRTEEN

The East Lobby meeting room was a rumble of activity, as thirty co-sponsors of the death penalty bill huddled about, along with the majority and minority leaders of the house, and the rest of the members. There was a cloud of both apprehension and anticipation that hung heavy overhead, as they anxiously awaited the appearance of the Codes Committee Chairman and his heads of staff to arrive.

Somehow, they all individually knew this meeting was going to make history, whether in their favor, or not.

They twiddled their fingers, replied to text messages, quietly engaged in conversation with those sitting to their left, or right. Heads simultaneously snapped to attention with precision, as Bryan entered the room with Connor and Jessica at his flank.

Quickly, Bryan scanned the faces of the men before him.

What a sorrowful lot, he thought. *If this is what it takes to see righteousness prevail, so be it*.

"Gentlemen, I'm sure you have some sense of why I've chosen to call you all here so urgently. I will not waste your time and cut to the chase. I'm tired of the rhetoric. Tired of washroom agreements and sucking someone's dick to push imperative issues through committees." There was a loud buzz in the room, but he spoke over it. "I was nominated and elected by down-home, hardworking people, who believe we're here to represent them in an honest fashion. I've been told to my face, that my bills will only see passage, if I jump through the hoops I'm directed too.

You see, gentlemen, if nothing else, I value my self-respect and falling asleep every night with a clear conscience. Many of you in this room can't say that."

The outburst could have lifted the roof from its rafters. He honestly expected the steam to burst from their ears and noses.

Good, he thought. *I've got their attention. Wait until they hear I'm sponsoring a bill to cut their terms to eight years.*

Bryan had it! The bastards, holding office for more than twenty years, were bankrupting this state, while filling their own coffers. There were thieves and swindlers sitting in front of him, puppets of oil barons, the top three insurance companies, and leading pharmaceuticals. It was time to clean the people's house of corruption.

"I will not plea bargain and, giving you sufficient notice. This matter is not up for discussion or a vote. My decision is irreversible. Either join my battle to take the death penalty to the people or drown on your own.

We've hacked at this issue for the past eight years. Like a repeating recording, we debate it to death, solving nothing, while innocent people are being murdered day after day. I will not continue to sit back and ignore what's happening around us. The public ... our people, gentlemen, are not only being killed, but butchered by crazed animals like the Luther Corbat's in this world. The number of deaths has climbed, and keep climbing by repeat offenders, who don't give a damn about human life.

The crazed, unstable, corrupted, and sadistic killers in our society laugh at justice in the face, because they know three square meals and a roof over their heads waits for them, not death.

I cannot nor will I turn a stone ear to my people. You keep doing so. I intend to do something now! I have called for a news conference first thing tomorrow morning in the Senate's conference room. If you support me, be there at 8:45. If not, too damn bad."

Bryan looked them all squarely in the eyes, then turned and departed, leaving them to talk amongst themselves, fume openly, or seek refuse in the privacy of their own offices.

The absolute quiet, which followed Sen. Gallagher's departure was uncanny. One could almost hear a pin drop and the wheels turning in the minds of the senate leaders occupying the room.

Sen. Martin Talbot stood up and cut through the silence in an authoritative tone.

"I truly envy, that young man. He had the balls to do, what many of us wanted to do for fucking years!" He chuckled lightly, as he ran his fingers through his thick, gray locks. His eyes scanned the faces of those colleagues sitting in front, to the side, and back of him.

He was a distinguished man in his mid-fifties and noted for his fair-game politics. He was one of those old timers, serving almost twenty years. He was also known as a man, who took shit from no one. His policies took a while to pass, but eventually did, without selling his soul to the devil.

Sen. Warren Shaughnessy was a man, who felt differently though, and didn't mind expressing his ire.

"Are you all fools? Come on! Have you no idea what the repercussions could be over this? Promises have been made and …"

"Sit down, Shaughnessy," Sen. Malcolm Scott shouted. He was Chairman of the Senate Ways & Means Committee. When he spoke, people listened. "We don't need to hear that shit. Marty's right, and you god damn well know it!" He was a robust man and his thick crop of greying, red hair matched his rising temper, as his cheeks flushed brightly. "Are we pissed? Yes. Why? Because he made us see a side to ourselves, we don't like."

"Still," Shaughnessy cut in, "how do we know supporting him is the right choice? Christ, man. A lot of those people out there take our word as gospel. Do we have the moral obligation to vote yes, if our constituency say no. Referendums are great for some things, not this. We're supposed to lead."

Sen. Maxwell Harriman laughed loudly, shaking his head and cut in.

"I don't believe this. You really think you're some kind of a god, for Christ's sake, don't you?" Harriman couldn't sit still any longer. He was a nervous sort and known to cover the floor, when debating an issue. Now, was no exception, as he rose. "Gallagher's not asking the people to press for a referendum.

He's going to tell them to put the pressure on us. It has started already!" He raised his cell phone to make a point. "Check with your own offices. The phones in mine are ringing off the frigging walls. Constituents are reacting on their own."

More members stood, nodding their heads in agreement, many speaking out, some louder than others, wishing to be heard.

Sen. Talbot cut through the bedlam with one of those shrilling whistle calls a parent would give in the old days, calling the kids home for the night. It worked as the room went silent and he got their attention.

"We were all elected by the people in our districts to represent them and their concerns. Ask yourselves. Have you? Do you? I don't know about the rest of you, but I will be there tomorrow, doing the right thing. If you're smart, you'll do the same."

CHAPTER FOURTEEN

Ever since the shooting hit the air waves, every Senate office was inundated with phone calls from constituents, local leaders, and religious activists. The callers in support of justice being served, outweighed those in opposition of the death penalty bill being passed. An "eye for an eye" was their cry. More than not, threatened not to support their representative's reelection in less than four weeks, if they did not abide to their wishes.

It wasn't long before the media heard about the leadership meeting. Quickly, they descended upon the Capitol with camera crews in tow, chasing down as many leaders as they could find for an interview.

Their attempts were futile, as members hid themselves behind closed doors, until they absolutely needed to make an appearance.

The public was going to see a side to Bryan, they never witnessed before. His speech could cause a tidal wave not seen on the plaza in quite some time. His return from the conference meeting was a solemn one. He informed his entire staff the moment he walked through the office, that he did not wish to be disturbed for any reason whatsoever. He expected them to hold the press at bay and relay he would hold all comments, until the press meeting the following morning.

No noise came from his inner sanctum. The board did not light up with outgoing calls being made, and the silence, he knew, was probably unnerving to his staff. He couldn't stave off the melancholy that hung over him like a heavy cloak. He felt terrible about what happened to Warren Michaelson, the officers transporting

Corbat, and the innocent woman, whose car the madman hijacked. The man was a demon, and there were many more like him, who senselessly killed those innocent individuals, who got in their way.

Bryan did not care, if he made enemies, or got ostracized for his beliefs. He was ready to take on the leadership, even if it proved to be all by himself.

This was the first time, that Jessica witnessed such solemnness from Bryan. She let him be. If he needed her, he'd buzz.

Everyone went about the operations of the office. Time flew rather quickly, as the staff stayed on top of the monster unleashed earlier. As soon as one call was extinguished, ten took its place. The concern ringing true throughout Bryan's own district was overwhelming. His constituents were behind him. It would give him great pleasure in knowing that.

"I think we ought to call it quits, Jessica, what do you say," Connor suggested, as he stepped into her office. "Seems the more we answer, the more they all keep calling. I'm going horse."

Jessica chuckled lightly. "Me too, and I'm sure the staff agrees. It's hopeless trying to keep up."

"You want me to tell them to shut down at 5:30?"

"Let Claire know first, and she can tell them. It's hopeless at this point. Ask her to call the switch board to take over."

Connor nodded. "I'll be right back," he replied and exited her office.

Jessica knew that tomorrow was going to be more chaotic than today even was. There would be no getting away from the press. All the major affiliates would be calling for personal interviews. It was all part of the game. The crazies would be coming out of the woodwork as well.

Connor returned and plopped into one of the visitor's chairs.

"Do you think we should check on Bryan and see if he's alright?" She asked.

Connor shrugged, looking a little bewildered.

"I was gonna ask you the same thing. I've never seen him like this before. I imagine he's preparing for tomorrow. I kind of expected him to call on us to help."

"Well, maybe he's confident about what he's going to say. Look, why don't you go? I'll stick around a while longer and poke my head in. Go home and have dinner with your wife and kids. I'll call you one way or the other, after I check on him. Okay?"

"Are you sure?"

"Just get out of here," she shewed him off with a wave of her hand, smiling.

"Thanks. Seems every night I get home later and later. It'll be nice to catch dinner with them. Make sure you call … I'll be waiting."

"I will … promise," she crossed her heart.

He exited her office and she absently looked at the door connecting her and Bryan's. The girls popped their heads in to say goodnight, as did Zachary and Nicholas, their intern. She took the next thirty minutes, to clear some paperwork off her desk and muddled over in her mind a few brief moments as to whether she should interrupt Bryan.

She mindlessly checked the time on her cell phone and decided the need to see him, was greater than having too. She rose, tiptoed over to the connecting door, and pressed her ear against the wood.

Nothing. Dead silence. She expected to hear music coming from the Pandora station he liked to listen too, or even the soft volume of news being reported on the CNN channel he always tuned into.

She scrunched her lips to the side of her mouth and turned back toward her desk. She took a step forward and bit down on her lower lip, as she tapped her foot reflectively, wondering whether she should disturb him. A moment passed, before she spun back around, placing her ear against the door one more time.

Before she could realize what was happening, the door swung open instantly. Jessica lost her balance and fell against Bryan's chest. She was never so embarrassed in her life. She snapped back like a tin soldier, her arms stiff at her side, and hesitantly lifted her head to meet his gaze.

He looked down at her, his eyebrow raised in question.

"Umm. You … you weren't supposed to do that," she uttered.

"I wasn't," he replied, a trace of a smile curving his lips. He reached out and encircled her waist, pulling her against him.

She could feel her cheeks blush with heat. The smell of his aftershave filled her nostrils and the rhythmic beating of his heart pounding against her breast excited her. A wanton desire stirred deep within her, and she tried to further explain her actions.

"You know what I mean, Senator," she squirmed, as she looked up into those gorgeous eyes of his.

She thought her knees would turn to liquid, as she read the same passion that was burning inside of her, reflected in their depths.

"It's after hours, Jessica. You don't have to call me Senator anymore."

She pressed her palms against his chest and could feel the tight muscles beneath his shirt. Just when she started to melt a little more and relax against him, the door to his office swung open.

"Well, looky here. Just as I expected, the tramp has got her claws into you, and I've only been gone a short while. Really, Bryan? I never expected you to be the type to screw your staff."

Before either of them could react, Angela closed the distance between them, pushed Jessica away, and wrapped Bryan in an iron embrace with a kiss, that would leave most men smoldering.

Bryan grabbed hold of her forearms and pushed her off him. "That's enough, Angela," he barked, stepping away. "There is no us, and you god damn well know it."

This was a scene Jessica refused to get pulled into and she spoke up immediately.

"I'll just leave you two to do whatever." She directed her attention toward Bryan. "Senator, I just wanted to tell you we're all set for the news conference in the morning. Connor and I will be in at seven to double-check and take care of anything that may arise from now, until then."

Angela stepped forward to do battle, but Bryan was quicker and placed himself between them.

Jessica respected his gallant attempt and smiled warmly. The look she sent Angela was pure disgust, and she spat out her true feelings.

"I'm too damned tired right now, to waste my breath and energy on you." She turned on her heel to leave and walked away.

"Worthless, bitch." Angela barked back right away.

Jessica looked over her shoulder and smugly retorted with a wave of her hand. "I'm here. You're not. That hair color, she pointed Angela's way, "looks way more attractive on me. Enough said. Night, Bryan. See you in the morning."

Bryan bristled after her and called out.

"Jessica wait." He reached for her, as she made it to the front lobby, and turned her about. "I'm sorry I didn't get a chance to connect with you and Connor today. I got engrossed with what I needed to prepare for."

"We know that" she replied softly, as she reached out to caress his cheek. "Are you ready? Do you need us to check anything over?"

He reached for her hand, pressed his lips to her fingertips, and held it against his chest. He shook his head confidently.

"I'm good. I really am. The input you both provided the other day helped considerably. He lowered his face and placed a long and tender kiss upon her lips. "Thank you."

She smiled. "You're most welcomed. I'll see you tomorrow." She jerked her head in the direction of his office. "Good luck with that one. You want me to call security and have her escorted out of here?"

He chuckled lightly. "No. I can handle her." He paused for a moment and his voice took on a more serious tone, as did his expression. "I can't tell you how happy I am to have you in my life." He wrapped his arms around her and drew her in, softly brushed his lips over hers and placed a tender kiss along the hollow of her neck. "There's so much more I want to say to you, Jessica, but now, is not the time. Have dinner with me tomorrow night?"

"Maybe we should wait and see how things turn out first, don't you think? I mean, all hell could break loose after the press conference."

"That's exactly, why I want to be with you. We can either share a last meal together, or we'll have reason to celebrate."

She laughed softly, shaking her head in amusement. "Alright then, it's a date." She planted a quick kiss upon his lips and opened the door to leave.

"Let CP know you need an escort to your car," he reminded her, as she stepped into the hallway.

She raised her cell phone for him to see and replied, "Yes, boss."

It was nearly seven in the evening, when her cell phone rang, and the caller id immediately placed a smile upon her face.

"Did you survive crazy lady? I take it there was no blood spilled?"

A warm and fuzzy feeling filled her up, when his laughter radiated from the speaker on her phone.

"She was a handful, but I managed to escape without any visual signs of injury."

"I'm pleased to hear that. Thank you for letting me know."

"It's not the only reason, why I called."

"Oh?" She answered in a surprised tone.

"I've got a craving for a hot fudge sundae. Care to join me?"

She didn't care if it was a sundae smothered in anchovies. She couldn't stop thinking about that kiss he dazzled her with, before leaving the office a few short hours ago.

"Mention chocolate, and I'm your girl." She replied happily.

"Cool! I'm outside your door."

Jessica couldn't help but laugh. She adored his confidence and the fact, that she was the person he thought of to call first.

"I'm on my way," she replied excitedly.

Jessica quickly ran a brush through her hair, threw on a pair of sweats, a zipped-up hoodie, sneakers and flew out of her room. She passed the library and noticed her aunt sitting by the fireplace reading and quickly popped her head inside.

"I'm on my way out for a short while to catch a hot fudge sundae with Bryan. Care for anything?"

The joy radiating on her aunt's face, was a clear indication of how pleased Florence was, that she was spending personal time with Bryan.

"Not a thing dear. You two enjoy."

When she opened the front door, he was there, leaning against the passenger side, his legs crossed at the ankles, and his hands very nonchalantly in his denim pockets. She realized then, it didn't matter what he wore. This man was hot! Her heart skipped in her chest … a regular occurrence, she also realized, whenever he was around. It was like she was sixteen all over again, and the hottest boy in school had a crush on her.

She hopped down the stairs and greeted him with a hug and kiss, as he enfolded her into his arms.

"I can't tell you how long it's been, since I had a sundae."

"I'm happy to be the reason for putting such a joyous smile on that gorgeous face of yours."

She punched him playfully in the shoulder.

"I bet you say that to all the girls."

He raised his right hand, and placed his open palm against her cheek, holding her face for a brief pause and replied honestly. "I adore only you."

Jessica couldn't help, but sigh deeply. It was juvenile, yes, but she just couldn't hold back how wonderful this man made her feel.

He pushed himself off the car and placed a tender kiss upon her nose, as he leaned over to open her door.

Jessica ducked her head, noticing a cooler on the back seat, and sat down quickly.

Bryan closed her door, before she had the chance to question, what he was up to.

"It's a surprise," he explained right away, "and no, I know that look. No questions. You'll just have to wait and see."

Jessica stuck out her tongue, making him chuckle heartily, as he turned on a great soft rock station, and placing the car in drive.

Once she got her bearings, Jessica was certain where Bryan was taking her. There was a popular, scenic, picnic spot, known as the "Overlook", where you could see the Empire State Plaza in the distance, along with the entire city. The accent lighting on the Plaza at night was rather attractive, and the city, even looked better at night. It was a very popular spot, especially during the special holidays, when all the fireworks colored the sky.

"Oh, my god! The last time I was here, was when Jimmy Callahan thought he could get some action after our Junior Prom." She looked at him and cut him off, before he could react. "And no," she added quickly, "he never made it to second base."

"Second, hah? Hmm."

She gave him that look, that plainly read, 'Not a chance, buster."

Not that she didn't want to see this man naked at some point in the very near future. God, just the thought of it had her insides shaking like a volcano nearing eruption. The growing passion between them was undeniable. The last thing she wanted though, was letting sex muddle her brain. She wanted to develop a lasting and binding connection with this man, and they were well on their way to doing just that.

Bryan walked to the back of his car and popped the trunk, responding, "Those green eyes of yours are very expressive, you know that?"

She followed him, noticing a small stack of firewood, and reached in for the remaining three logs he wasn't carrying.

"I've been told that, yes, many times." She followed him to where a fire pit, had been dug out of the ground. He took the logs from her arms. "This was such a great idea, Bryan. I got a feeling we're making our own sundaes, right?"

"You got it. I brought along a jacket for us both, in case we get a little chilly. There's a blanket in the trunk. Mind getting it, while I grab the cooler in the backseat?"

Jessica nodded and did just that.

In a matter of minutes, Bryan had a nice fire burning next to the blanket they had spread out, overlooking the view. It was a glorious fall night. There wasn't a cloud hiding not even one of the thousands of stars twinkling overhead. He hadn't forgotten a thing, as he emptied the cooler of its contents. There was also a small wicker carrier, containing a chilled bottle of Riesling and two plastic wine glasses. Since, he wasn't certain what flavor of ice cream she preferred, he had a half-gallon of vanilla, strawberry, and chocolate along with all the toppings they needed, including whipped cream, nuts, cherries, hot fudge, caramel, marshmallow, and of course, colorful sprinkles.

It was glorious, and yummy, and romantic, and entertaining, and the dates of all dates ever. When Richard came into her life, they always dined at the most expensive restaurants accompanied by another couple, but never alone. They attended lavish galas, where they could be seen, and hob-knobbing with the rich and famous. Not once, were they ever alone. She was always in the presence of others.

With Bryan, it was different. She got to know the man, his most inner thoughts, his hopes and dreams. This moment was a topper. And the best of all, was the kisses between each spoonful … kisses dabbled with whipped cream, or smudges of hot fudge. They shared in quick ones, in between conversation ones, and the ones she loved and craved more of were the long, melting, steamy ones, that pulled her deeper and deeper into a world of heated passion.

She let him get to second base, and really, really, close to third.

He made sure, that the night air, did not chill her exposed skin, not even once.

CHAPTER FIFTEEN

The public hearing room was packed with every tv. crew from the entire capital district region. Equipment was set at every available spot and stood in ready for Bryan's public address to the state.

The press conference was open to the public as well. Representatives from community groups, clergy, and the public in all denominations filled the one-thousand seats of the auditorium in record time. Banners and signs were waving with sentiments in large, bold letters that read

'D.P. FOREVER, 'PUNISHMENT FOR THE UNJUST'. 'FRY THOSE WHO KILL', 'NEW YORK WANTS THE DEATH PENALTY.'

Anyone uncertain, as to the reason for the gathering, would most probably think a demonstration was in progress. There was a low din of chants, that could be heard. The suspense and excitement climbed, as members themselves, began to mill in from the closely-guarded private entrance to the right side of the room.

The light fixtures hovering over the solid mahogany dais floor became ablaze in light as Sen. Gallagher's entourage filtered in. The house broke out into pandemonium, as onlookers applauded and cheered. Chants echoed the air, claps roared in unison, banners and signs waved and rose in excited accord.

Bryan's pulse pounded like the hooves of racehorse closing in on the finish line, as his eyes scanned the faces of those in attendance. The members he addressed just the other day were there in support. It was a packed house with standing room only.

Connor stood to his right, while Jessica stood to his left. Without thinking, Bryan reached out for her hand, and she did not hesitate to entwine her fingers with his.

He had spoken in front of larger crowds before. This speech though, was going to be a pivotal one in his career, because a national stage was being set by the networks in front of him. What New York decided, other states would more than likely follow.

Bryan gave himself a moment to let it all sink in, as he carefully looked at everyone in the room. He wanted them to know he saw them and acknowledged them with a nod. Some of their faces mirrored awe, excitement, tearful rejoice, and yes, those in opposition. Then, there was one, one, that made Bryan stop, take notice, and focus on him individually.

A hateful rage emanated from the man, standing to the left of his podium, not even two feet away. There was something about him, that seemed familiar. He was casually, but slovenly attired. His long hair looked greasy and tied back into a tail. And then it dawned on him, as he poked Connor at his side, noticing the thickly, framed, black bifocal glasses.

His look of recognition, prompted a slow, knowing sneer upon the stranger's face.

Bryan turned to Connor and whispered loudly.

"To our left. See the short, rounded guy with his hair in a ponytail and the thick glasses.?"

"You mean the one heading for the door," Connor nodded.

Bryan turned his head quickly to see, and damn sure, the guy was bolting for the door. Bryan waved for the attention of a Capitol Police Officer standing nearby, and the officer quickly neared.

"The guy, heading for the door. I'm damn sure he's the one, who attacked one of my staff members a few weeks ago."

The Officer didn't waste a moment and bolted off the dais in pursuit.

Bryan wanted to take the attention of what had just happened off the pursuing officer. He loudly cleared his throat and rose his arms to gain the attention of the crowd.

"Ladies and gentlemen, please." He spoke loudly into the microphone before him.

Silence was almost immediate, and Bryan proceeded in a calm and confident voice.

"Thank you all for coming here today, whether it be in support, or opposition to my cause. It is with a heavy heart, that first, I must share a call I just received from Gov. Michaelson just moments ago. Sadly, his son, Warren, has passed away."

A deafening uproar filled the air, as the attendees expressed their sorrow, and calls for revenge.

Bryan slapped the gavel upon it's block before him, beseeching their attention.

"Please … please … a moment. No," he shook his head and waved his hand, as reporters vied for his attention. "No questions, yet please. I ask that we pause for a moment, in silent prayer, for the soul of Trooper Warren Michaelson and his grieving family."

Respectfully, the noise slowly decreased, as heads bowed in silence for the brief, moment requested.

Bryan raised his eyes to gaze over the crowd before him, and again he noticed the individual from before, this time standing all the way towards the back of the room. The hair at the back of his neck prickled, as the man leered back at him with such derision, he expected him to pull out a gun. As Bryan looked about for another Officer, the stranger turned and bolted from the room.

He decided to carry on, but continued his vigilance, as his eyes continually scanned the entire room.

"As you all know; I am sponsoring the death penalty bill."

Bedlam broke out once again, overriding the small religious group, who were expressing their opposition.

"Yes, I know many of you disagree. However, the public outcry has been expeditious in support. It is not my colleagues I represent here. It is not the judges, the mayors of our cities, the leaders of our town boards I listen to. It is you, the people of my district, the parents of fallen victims, the families of our public servants gunned down by these senseless killers I listen to and represent, and you in this room, who cry out for justice today."

He gave the people in the room a moment to react, before he continued.

"Because of the seriousness of this legislation, I beseech the support of my colleagues on both sides of the aisle in the Senate and Assembly. I cannot emphasize how important it is, that you, the blue-collar worker, the professional, and the laborer reach out to your representatives and express your support. Most of you have felt your concerns are never heard. That may be true on a small scale, but if a mass majority of voices are spoken, they must listen. Three-fourths of this State's population want this legislation law.

Why do my colleagues vote it down, you ask, year after year? Tell them to do their job. Tell them to represent your vote and your voice. Our aunts and uncles, our sisters and brothers, our parents and grandparents, our sons and daughters are being victimized. They are being brutally, viciously, and senselessly murdered. It needs to stop, and I need your help. I can't do it alone. Make your support known today! We can do it this year … this legislative session," he pointed at them emphatically.

"We need to let the criminal element out there know, that killing someone will not go unpunished. We need to take back control and put the word out on the streets, that our justice system is no longer soft on murder, the days of a cot for life and three-square meals a day are over. The free ride for life ends <u>here</u> and ends <u>now</u>.

Thank you all for coming here today and actively being a part of this State's legislative process."

Reporters bustled closer to the podium, trying to draw attention to their questioning.

"Senator Gallagher, please," Ross Chandler for WSAC News. "You must feel a little jubilant, knowing your bill will become a law after all these years?"

Bryan replied immediately. "You must know something, I don't, Ross."

"Ah, come on Senator," the reporter pushed. "The Governor's son has just been snuffed by a convicted killer. It's like money in the bank for you."

Bryan's tone was irritated.

"Okay, that was heartless and rather crass to presume the Governor will change his stand, because he just lost his son."

Questions flew at him from all directions.

"Senator, who were your colleagues, who misrepresented their voters? Do you think Luther Corbat will be executed now? Is the bill still in committee?"

Bryan raised his hands to stay further questioning.

"The bill is on the Codes agenda for a vote as we speak. As far as my colleagues are concerned, their votes are public record. Those in support, stand behind me now," he nodded over his shoulder. "If it goes to the floor, you'll be on that voting list like bees to honey."

Laughter broke out amongst them, as assurance, he was right.

Yancy Hamilton News 10 rose her hand.

"Yes, Yancy," Bryan acknowledged.

"Senator, do you plan to meet with the Governor to discuss, or perhaps negotiate, what to do with the Luther Corbat's out there?"

"My priority," he answered, "is to express my deepest condolences in person. I don't plan to bring up the subject. Now, if you all will excuse me, I have a lot of work to do. Again, thank you all for coming."

Bryan turned toward Jessica and lightly encircled her waist with his arm, and with Connor by his other side, they exited the public hearing room together.

They halted just outside the door, in a small anti-room.

Connor was the first to speak, with a pleased look upon his face.

"That went well, don't you think?"

Bryan nodded and replied.

"I'm happy with the membership, who showed. It wasn't the majority though. We'll have to wait and see, if the public puts the pressure on."

"Well, you know you'll be the headline news tonight, and I think the numbers will surprise you."

Bryan shrugged. "Time will tell. Look, I can't thank the two of you enough. We've put in a lot of long hours over the last few weeks. I'm confident we've got the majority vote to get it out of committee. I'd like the two of you to join me tonight for dinner. Connor, how about Abigail? Do you think she can get a sitter on such short notice?

Connor pulled his cell from his breast jacket pocket. "I'll give her a call now," he replied, and walked away to make the call.

Bryan looked at Jessica and pulled her to the side.

"Why don't you head on up. I need to talk to the Sergeant over there, "he nodded in the direction of the officer standing a few feet away.

"Anything serious," she asked in a concern filled tone.

"Nothing for you to be worried about," he replied.

Connor returned. "Abigail can join us. I told her I would give her the details later."

"Great," Bryan answered. "You two head back. I'll catch up with you shortly."

Jessica looked at him, as though she surmised something else was up, but hesitated only briefly and turned to walk with Connor.

Bryan directed his attention to the Sergeant and closed the distance between them.

"Senator, what can I do for you? You've got that look on your face, that something isn't quite right."

He knew Sergeant Taft a long time. Mac was on foot patrol for the city for almost five years, before he switched over to the Capitol Police. He rose in the ranks quickly then.

"It's not, Mac. That man I sent one of your officers after, I'm certain was the same guy, who accosted Jessica on my staff."

The Sergeant's look wasn't a happy one either. "You're dead certain."

"Enough for a line up. I think, if we pull the tape from the camera in there that was directed at the dais, we'll find that the guy standing less than two feet away from us on my left, was the bastard that attacked Jessica outside my office."

"I'll go pull it right away, run them side-to-side and see if you're right. Give me a few hours to get back to you."

Bryan reached out his hand to acknowledge his offer. "Thanks, Mac. I'll be around only until about 5:30, and then I'll be out for the evening. After that, you have my cell."

"Will do, Senator. I'll take care of this myself."

"Thanks, Mac."

CHAPTER SIXTEEN

Now, Bryan had cause for concern. He looked at the coffee cup, that had been sitting on his desk, since five o'clock that morning. Its contents were cold from being ignored. He didn't need it to stay awake. Sleep had been evading him for quite some time now. Last night was no exception. He, just, couldn't fall to sleep for shit. He tossed and turned for nearly four hours, until finally he gave up, when the digital time on his bedside clock read 4:15 a.m.

He should have fallen right to sleep too. He had two glasses of wine at dinner, a delicious meal, and relaxing conversation. Abigail and Jessica hit it off, as though they had known each other forever. He kept checking his phone for a text or voice message from Mac. He never heard back from him, until well after ten o'clock last night.

The news Mac shared, hadn't been good. He confirmed, just what Bryan had suspected all along. The man, who accosted Jessica her first day on the job, was the same guy at yesterday's press conference.

At least, he knew what he was dealing with. There was no doubt left in his mind, that this was a personal vendetta. It had everything to do with his sponsorship of the death penalty bill, some close friend/family member sitting on death row, or both.

He knew this guy was planning something ... watching them. The question was, was he the target, or would this bastard go after Jessica again? He knew in his heart it would be the latter. He'd bet his seat in the Senate on it. He wasn't a shrink, but his professional experience told him, that this guy was a psychopath. He got a thrill out of being covert and scheming out his next attack.

Bryan's sponsorship of the death penalty bill somehow tripped something in this guy, to the point he was compelled to fight back, to lash out on behalf of someone close to him. He targeted Jessica out of sheer, unbridled cruelty, for the enjoyment of creating fear and making her suffer.

The public knew by now, that his engagement had been severed with Angela. The sicko knew by now, that Jessica was never his fiancé. But, being a member of his staff, placed a target on her back, and this guy saw her standing beside him at the press conference yesterday.

Bryan knew, he had to do everything in his power to protect her. Even though he knew her barely two months, she had stolen his heart. He would die, if any harm came to her. He also knew, he had to let Florence know as well. She was in jeopardy too, since Jessica was living under her roof. He wouldn't be surprised, if this madman had been following Jessica all along.

He had also heard from Dante. There wasn't any banter out on the streets about this guy either. Not one word, even after, Bryan told Dante he'd pay five-hundred dollars to anyone with sound information.

Clearly, this guy never had dealings of any kind with those thugs … again, a validation he was a loner.

The screen shot pulled from the security tapes of the press meeting didn't match anything in the system, frustrating the piss out of him, even more. It would have made finding him, so much easier.

It was time to call in reinforcements, and Bryan picked up his cell to call his old partner of almost five years, Ayden Tyler.

"Shit, man. You know what time it is?" Ayden answered groggily on the second ring.

"Sorry to wake you, bud. It's real important."

Bryan could hear the rustle of covers and the click of a table lamp go on in the background.

"Spill."

"I've got a psycho on my tail, who made a move on one of my staff. I need your help finding this bastard."

He heard the click of a lighter and Ayden taking a drag on the other end.

"What do you know so far?"

"Well, first, I was wondering, if you could stop by my office … any time after two I'm open. We can talk then."

"You got time now? All I gotta do is zip up my fly."

Bryan chuckled. He missed Ayden's wit. It kept the sanity real, when things got rough out on the streets. "I'm free until ten. The coffee is fresh and hot."

"On my way."

"Thanks, man."

Bryan called down to the front desk to let the officers on duty know Ayden was on his way in and would be carrying.

Ayden was sitting comfortably in front of Bryan with his feet propped up on his desk, sipping a freshly brewed cup of coffee less than twenty minutes after they first talked.

"This is bonkers, Bry. I still can't wrap my mind around you being a Senator." He admitted openly, as his eyes did a quick loop around the office.

"Neither can I. I miss working the streets and interrogating perps with you."

"Your snitch ... Dante, you believe him?"

Bryan took a sip of his fresh brew and nodded.

"I do. This guys a loner. I just know it."

"You said the Trooper's took this over. They come up with anything."

"Haven't heard a thing. I need to dig, Ayden. I can't sit around like this waiting for him to make his next move."

"So, what's ours?"

"Court tapes," Bryan offered. "Do you still know that pretty court clerk? I've got a feeling this guy was in the courtroom, during the Corbat trial. None of this shit happened, until he was found guilty. I need us to get our hands on the security tapes during that entire trial. I know, as sure as we're sitting here, that prick, who attacked Jessica, was there too."

"If he was we've a good chance figuring out what the connection between him and Corbat is. And it just so happens, Samantha still works there. I'll stop by for a visit, as soon as the doors open."

Bryan stood and walked around his desk, his hand extended in thanks.

Ayden placed his empty coffee cup on Bryan's desk, clasped Bryan's hand, and they drew each other in for a 'man hug.'

"We'll get this guy, Bry. Don't you worry."

"I'm counting on it." He replied.

Just as Jessica opened the front office door, Ayden was exiting Bryan's office, with Bryan following close behind. She jumped with a start, never expecting anyone to be at the office before her, especially at this hour. She noticed the dark circles under Bryan's eyes immediately and knew something had to be up. The badge clipped on the belt buckle of the handsome gentleman standing before her, quickly caught her attention as well.

"My lord, you're in early." She directed her remark to Bryan. "Pressing business?"

Bryan was quick to answer.

"Jessica this is a real close buddy of mine and former partner for nearly five years, Det. Ayden Tyler. Ayden, this is my Dir. Of Communications, Jessica Wilton."

Jessica knew there was something amiss. She could tell by the look on Bryan's face … like a little boy caught with his hand in the cookie jar. She clasped a hold of the Detective's extended hand.

"It's nice to make your acquaintance, Ms. Wilton." He offered and released her hand, nodding respectfully. He quickly stepped to the side and nodded at Bryan. "See you soon, Bry. It's time for another steak dinner. My treat this time, remember."

"I never forget, when it's your turn to pay."

Both men chuckled and the Detective was quickly gone.

She couldn't hide the concern in her voice.

"You look downright exhausted. Have you been here all night?"

He shook his head.

"Slept, no. Here since just before 5."

She took off her leather coat and hung it in the front closet.

"You want to tell me what's bothering you? It's about that madman, isn't it?"

"What makes you think that?"

"Haven't you learned yet, that women are supremely intuitive?"

His dimple was so pronounced, she just wanted to plant her lips right there, on that same exact spot. She knew he was keeping that incident under wraps, because he didn't want to scare and upset her. It irked her a little. She wasn't that scared little girl anymore. She knew how to shoot a gun and defend herself.

He changed the subject right away.

"I needed some quiet time, that's all. Ayden and I have been trying to connect for weeks, and this was kind of on the fly and worked for both of us. Yes, we talked a little bit about what happened. I still need you to be careful and not go off alone around here, until this guy is caught."

She followed him into his office and occupied the chair Ayden had been in earlier. She noticed his coffee cup on Bryan's desk, stood up, and placed it on the credenza where the Keurig was. She looked over her shoulder and asked, "Care for another cup?"

Bryan shook his head no and she went through the rudiments of fixing herself one.

"Since we're both here early, want to go over what's on the calendar for today?"

He moved quietly up behind her and slowly turned her around, interlacing his fingers at the curve of her back.

"I know one thing I'd like to address first."

She smiled knowingly but went along anyways.

"And, what's that, Senator."

"This," he replied, softly claiming her lips.

She melted … like butter over a slow heat and got lost in the wonder of his lips caressing hers. Every kiss they shared was better than the one before. Even his goodnight kiss, when he walked her to her car, was now just a memory, a beautiful one, nonetheless. But it was being replaced by a softer, more tortuous, and hypnotic exploration.

He knew how to explore her mouth, without being invasive. He knew how to tantalize her senses, without being soppy, and he knew how to stir passion's fire, leaving her wanting more of the same.

It was six-thirty, when she first arrived. She remembered Connor saying over dinner he planned on coming in that morning around seven, and she didn't want him finding them in a lover's embrace. As much as she hated being the one to break the spell between them, she pulled away, with an honest excuse passing from her lips. She heard the breathlessness in her voice and blushed.

"Connor will be here soon."

He kissed her softly one last time and drew away, walking back to his chair, and sitting down.

She turned back to retrieve her coffee, opened two packets of cream, and stirred the contents, as she blew out a breath very slowly. The aftereffects of his kiss left her slightly shaken and she wrapped both of her hands around her coffee cup, and took the seat in front of him.

"Now, about today," she proceeded, making him chuckle lightly. She smiled at his reaction and continued. "I don't know, if you remember or not, I scheduled myself for the tour of the Capitol at noon. If that's still, okay?"

She could tell he was mulling that over in his mind a little too long. She noticed his forehead furrowing slightly with concern and argued the point before he did.

"I know what you're thinking, Bryan, and you don't have to worry. There's safety in numbers, and the Tour Office already confirmed there will be 25 other people in attendance. I am really, looking forward to it. It'll be somewhat slow around here today and the tour is only an hour long. There's a possibility it may go over by thirty minutes, depending on how many questions everyone has along the way."

She didn't say anything else. She was confident her argument was strong enough. It took him only a few more moments to reply.

"Enjoy yourself. I'll have lunch ordered around one-thirty for the three of us. You said the Today Show confirmed my interview with Matt Lauer this Friday at 9 a.m., correct?"

"Yes, that's right. They sent me a list of questions for approval. I've already finished writing out your responses and we can go over them when I return."

"That's why I love ya. You know what I'm thinking, before I do."

"Oh, not on all matters," she jested playfully.

CHAPTER SEVENTEEN

The Capitol served, as the seat of New York's government, since the 1880's. Jessica knew the building was completed maybe a decade after that at a cost of around twenty-million. That was the extent of her knowledge, however. As much as she wanted to learn more, working for Bryan kept her terribly busy. What excited her most, was learning about the famous 'Million Dollar Staircase,' she climbed nearly every day.

There were already fifteen people congregated in the public tour section, awaiting the arrival of their appointed guide and the remaining group members. Jessica smiled at a couple, who she thought were in their early sixties. She noticed most of those milling about were seniors, all of whom took turns saying hello.

In a matter of minutes, the remaining ten arrived together, all high school teenagers, along with their chaperone. The tour guide made her entrance shortly, thereafter, garbed in a well-tailored two-piece navy pant suit, complimented by a blue and red starred ascot tied about her neck. She was an adorable individual, dainty and petite of frame with a pleasant speaking voice.

"Hello, everyone. My name is Melinda Wentworth. On behalf of the State of New York, welcome to our State Capitol. If you have any questions during our tour, please feel free to speak up. I'll do my very best to answer any you may have. Let's begin, as we make our way toward our first stop."

Everyone proceeded quietly behind in an orderly manner, their eyes already scanning the area around them.

"The tremendous weight of these majestic granite walls," she pointed, "were originally constructed for the grand tower left uncrowned that you see above us. Nearly a quarter of a century passed, until Gov. Alfred E. Smith began the restoration of the lower part of the tower to something like it was originally designed. The second floor, you'll see," she directed their eyes, "was removed to create a rotunda forty-feet high and made into this Flag Room we're now entering."

The room was tall, to say the least, and held Civil War keepsakes encased in glass. It included a huge collection of the State's flags from the very beginning of statehood. The arched ceiling overhead depicted murals of historic wars. The most focal piece in the center, was an embossed female figure of a woman mourning the dead.

"A New York artist named William DeLeftwich Dodge," the guide continued, as she slowly moved along, "was commissioned to paint the artwork you see here. He spent five years putting twenty-four panels of canvas in his home studio, aided by his daughter Sara, while the erection of the domed ceiling was finished. Finally, in 1928, it was ready, and the murals were attached."

The group took a moment to check out the artifacts, and then moved on to the freight elevator, which took them to the second floor. Slowly, they made their way down the Hall of Governors. Upon its walls, hung huge oil paintings of New York's former governors, from beginning too present.

The Governor's official 'Red Room' was next on their stop. Everyone were awed by the rich fabrics and fixtures, and the highly-polished woods that gleamed ageless in his chambers. For some reason, this room brought out their cell phones, as they utilized their cameras to mark the moment.

Jessica noticed that a newcomer joined their group upon their exiting the Red Room. He seemed so out of place and acted terribly nervous. It was like he didn't want to be there, and she could tell his skinny frame was shaking. He was a mousy sort of fellow and hung back from the rest of the spectators, almost as if, he intended not to follow along.

Jessica found herself repeatedly looking over her shoulder. When she did, she found him watching her, instead of taking interest in the artifacts and historical references being brought to their attention.

They passed through thick double-glassed doors, which she knew lead to the Senate Chambers. Melinda continued her monolog, as everyone circled around her.

"H.H. Richardson was responsible for this Chamber's design. This is where our legislative leaders in the Senate conduct their business, while in session. Mr. Richardson began his work with limitations though, due to construction commitments made years before him. He had the same amount of space, as the Assembly Chambers to work with. But he didn't need it all, since the Senate numbered fewer in members. Back then, there were 128 members of the Assembly and only 32 Senators. So, he created the East Lobby adjacent to us, and a West Lobby at the farther end of the room."

Jessica agreed, it was a magnificent area with its gothic arches and carpeting, that reflected the numerous colors in the stained-glass windows. The solid brass chandeliers, wall sconces and lamps, Bryan had told her, while sitting in the chambers, were replicas of original gas fixtures from the past. Her attention was drawn to the golden oak ceiling overhead, with its beautiful craftsmanship, and wood panels. The walls were made of stone in a variety of onyx, marble, and granite throughout.

Her chest puffed with pride. She had the honor and privilege of entering this room many times.

"You can see up there," their guide pointed, "galleries were constructed for the public to visit and watch the proceedings here below. Mr. Richardson thrilled in using imports from all over the world. The walls, pillars and arches are Mexican onyx. The fireplaces were built with Siena marble. The chairs and settees were made of Spanish leather; and Caribbean red-brown mahogany was used for the desks."

As they began to leave through the West Senate lobby, she moved to the side to call Bryan on her cell. She wanted to make sure he didn't need her back for anything pressing. There was still the staircase to view, and she didn't want to miss it.

Bryan assured her all was well and not to worry. She caught up with the procession almost immediately. She noticed that the odd ball, who had joined them much later, was missing from the group. She turned about to see, if he was lagging, and was startled, as she caught him jumping behind one of the massive marble pillars to hide himself.

That's strange! She exclaimed silently, making a face. *Is he that shy for Pete's sake?*

For a moment, she thought his actions were just too bizarre and thought about warning the Sergeant-of-Arms, as to his odd behavior.

The Tour Guide's cry, "Our next stop is the million-dollar staircase," caught Jessica's attention. She shrugged her concern off and hurried to close the distance between her and the group.

No matter how many times she had climbed this staircase already, she always found it to be a wondrous masterpiece.

Melinda explained how it was a correlation between Moorish and Victorian Gothic, whatever that meant. What Jessica saw, was an intricate series of elegant arches. The carvings in the wood, were exquisite designs. No two were alike and Melinda further explained how they depicted the scale of evolution, as the staircase ascended.

There was a nine-foot wheel, that to her looked like a rose-window, set within the balustrade between the third and fourth levels.

"Red Corse hill sandstone, which is a freestone commonly used for fine carving, was imported from Scotland," Melinda explained. "When it's first quarried, it's soft and hardens slowly the more it's exposed to the air. After it's rubbed out, it resembles the polished wood you see here. It worked out so well on the Senate staircase, it became the principal stone for the entire Great Western Staircase, which was popularly nicknamed the 'Million-Dollar"

Staircase," she opened her arms wide, smiling proudly. "The actual cost, fell in the neighborhood, of one-million-five-hundred thousand dollars.

This staircase measures seventy-seven feet and one-hundred-nineteen feet up to the skylight above. A steam engine in the attic hoisted the stone for construction. It took twice as long to build, because there were periodic layoffs due to lack of funds, lasting five and a half years."

It was then, that Jessica noticed the mass of carvings, being pointed out, as they continued to climb. The fact that the Civil War was still very vivid in the minds of the craftsmen, its hero's faces were carved here ... Lincoln, Generals Grant and Sherman. Melinda also pointed out John Brown, Harriet Beecher Stowe, and the mulatto abolitionist, Frederick Douglass. A poet's corner, also honored Whitman, Longfellow, and Whittier."

Their guide chuckled softly, as she continued. "Legends have it, that the heads no one couldn't identify, were actually, those relatives and friends of the carvers. A half-dozen remained unidentified. These two though," she pointed out, "are the daughter and granddaughter of Isaac Perry, one of the major stone carvers of the staircase."

They climbed the last final steps to the sixth-floor landing, and she counted them to herself quietly.

Thirty-eight, thirty-nine, forty, she gasped aloud. She could tell many of the seniors were breathless and scurried to occupy the leather benches and chairs scattered about for the public's relaxation.

Melinda went from guest-to-guest, thanking them one last time for joining the tour, and answered whatever lingering questions they might have.

Jessica heard one of the seniors telling another it was just one o'clock. She knew that Bryan was going to have lunch delivered around one-forty-five. It was the first time, that she was ever up on the sixth floor and she looked about. Two of the seniors, who stayed by her side the duration of the tour, said their goodbyes.

Jessica watched as the entire group of them made their way onto the elevator with the guide and she waved to them, as the doors slowly began to close. The teens and their chaperone decided to take the stairs back down to the main floor.

Jessica thought to herself, *Good for them*, and watched, as they enthusiastically began to descend the staircase, until they were out of sight.

She turned and decided to follow the corridor to her right. She had no idea where it would take her and let her curiosity lead the way. It did not take long for the echoing sounds of the teens to disappear the further on she walked.

Soon, silence permeated around her. It became rather obvious; the sixth floor hadn't been used in a very long time. It even smelled musty, the farther she walked. She didn't hear any distant chatter, or those normal noises a busy office generated. It was somewhat eerie in a way, and Jessica found herself questioning her decision to be up here by herself.

A breeze wafted over her, and she shivered, wondering where it may have originated from. There were no open windows or doorways, that she could see, as she turned yet, another corner. It was a short walkway, that soon curved to the left. It seemed like her shoulder bag was getting heavier and she readjusted it like a bullet bandolier across her chest.

"Where the heck does this lead?" She spoke aloud.

She entered another chamber, which seemed virtually endless. This floor was all unused space. She knew that once the Legislative Office Building was constructed, most of the Senate and Assembly offices were transferred to there, leaving, a majority, of the Capitol empty. An entire empty floor was haunting.

She tested many of the doors and found that they were all locked. She couldn't tell whether the sounds of footsteps echoing around her were still hers, or those of someone else.

Even the sound of her own breathing, vibrated loudly, making the hairs prickle on the back of her neck. She strained her ears to pick up any background noise, but it was only the silence that greeted her.

The more she walked, the more uncomfortable she became. The light in the room seemed to start to fade as well. Jessica quickly glanced at her phone.

"Shit!" She muttered, as she noticed only one bar remained. She became irritated … extremely so. She should have returned to the office, instead of venturing into the unknown like this.

"Damn it," she scoffed, stomping her foot in aggravation.

She knew she had just bitten through the skin of her lower lip from the metallic taste of blood in her mouth. An unsettling feeling washed over her, and it was then, she decided to retrace her steps.

Were her eyes, playing tricks on her? Was the light beginning to fade?

She dialed Bryan's number right away, but he did not pick up. She decided to text him instead, before her phone died completely.

Hey, Bryan. The tour ended forty-five minutes earlier. I decided to check out the sixth floor. What a mistake. My phone's about to die. I'm on my way back now.

She put her phone on Airplane Mode to conserve her battery power.

She knew she was still a short distance away from the elevators and hurried her steps. She was anxious to get back to the office. She heard scampering noises, coming from the vents overhead and knew it had to be rodents. She shuddered and fear, for some reason, started to prickle at her brain. She could feel her heart beating harder against her chest, as beads of perspiration dotted her upper lip.

This was such a stupid idea, she chastised herself quietly.

Her phone let off a tone, signaling it was shutting down due to low voltage. She huffed loudly, shaking her head with annoyance, as she shoved it inside her shoulder bag. Bryan would never let her forget this. She knew she was late now, and he was probably getting worried. She rounded the corner and yelped out loud, startled by the person standing in front of her.

It was the lanky, young man from the tour, who had been acting strangely. But what struck the most fear in her heart, was the figure of the man, who just turned the corner.

She knew she wouldn't be returning to the office, as she gazed upon the face of her attacker the first day she started with Bryan's office.

CHAPTER EIGHTEEN

"We meet again," he cackled, as though mightily pleased with himself.

He took a step closer.

She took three steps back.

A chill ran through her, as her eyes darted about the room. There was no avenue of escape. The last thing she needed to do, was turn around and run, back into that maze of corridors and locked doorways. She knew she just had to be close to the elevators. She thought about the revolver tucked safely away at the bottom of her shoulder bag. By the time she dug it out though, they'd be on her, and fast.

Jessica knew it was smarter not to give away the fact she was concealing and hoped they wouldn't attempt to take her bag away from her. She kept her hands at her side, even though she wanted to cradle the bag protectively.

"It's obvious you want something, so, what is it?" She replied dryly.

The tall, lanky kid beside the villainous lout looked nervous as hell. If she was a betting woman, she'd guess he was no older than twenty-years old. His eyes darted about, and he shuffled nervously. He was either coerced into being there, or threatened within an inch of his life, based on the visible bruises she noticed coloring his cheeks and wrists.

She had to keep her wits about her, if she wanted to survive. It was something she had experience at doing. This time, she was smarter and better trained at defending herself. She looked the lanky boy up and down.

I can take him. She surmised with confidence.

She looked back at the filthy lump at the kid's side and knew, if she kicked him forcibly in the gut, he'd hit the ground hard gasping for breath.

The fat lard surprised her then, reaching his right hand around behind him.

Damn! Her mind screamed, as she looked down the barrel of a 357 being pointed straight at her chest.

She hadn't expected that, at all. It changed the dynamics, but she wasn't about to let the fear tapping at her insides, get the best of her. She still had the element of surprise on her side … well, two elements, actually. She too had a gun, and she could whip their asses.

He smiled slowly at her cockiness and rubbed his jawline, heavy with a few days' growth.

"You're gonna be my … my tool of persuasion, missy."

"And why would I want to do that?"

He waved the revolver like a flag and remarked smartly.

"Because this fucking gun speaks for me."

"Sy! Damn it, man. You never said –"

The man, now known as Sy, reached out and slapped the boy forcibly across the face, knocking him backwards.

"Shut the fuck up! You do, as I say, hear?"

The alarm planted on the young man's face created a flash of sympathy inside her towards him. There was a chance, she realized, that she might convince him to help her, and work his plight in her favor.

She didn't let Sy's lashing out rile her. She crossed her arms at her chest and waited to see, if he would answer her. Her calm patience won over and he acquiesced.

"You're a real smart one, aren't ya?"

Jessica sighed and clapped her palms tenderly together, as if in prayer.

"I think it's only fair for me to know, why you're doing this and what purpose it would serve. Wouldn't you, Sy, if you were in my shoes?" She pushed.

Her tender usage of his name made his head snap slightly.

Jessica tried to remember what her self-defense instructor taught her about situations just like this.

She knew this could turn deadly and her survival would be based on the decisions she made from this point forward. She had to keep her wits about her and calm down. She knew she was going to be abducted and what she was about to hear, clarified it.

"I know that high and mighty Senator you work for, is real sweet on you. I saw the way he looked at you … touched you. It got my mind to thinking. If I had you in my custody, well … that fucking death penalty bill of his, wouldn't go nowhere. He'd be forced to put it aside, and forget about it."

So, that was it. He was going to use her as leverage. She was safe for now. There was room for negotiation, room for her to work on him, maybe talk him out of this, and time … time to possibly figure out how to escape, once she learned where he would be taking her.

"Is someone you love … someone you care about serving time on death row? Look," she pressed further, "if you feel they're not guilty, I swear, I can help you win a stay of execution and – "

"My fucking brother deserves to rot in hell!"

She was confused and her expression surely mirrored that.

"Then, why? I … I don't understand."

Spittle ran from the corner of his mouth and down his chin, as his eyes grew large with the rage that welled from deep inside of him. His reaction caused her to take another step back, and the young man beside him, did the same.

"Because my fucking name will be ruined. Because the name Corbat is the reason, he's pushing the fucking bill. That's why! I already got fired because of it. I ain't gonna allow him to use my brother as his ticket to the Governor's Mansion. That's fucking why, bitch!"

She knew there wasn't going to be any rationalizing with this madman. He had blinders on and viewed passage of Bryan's bill, as a reason why his personal life turned to shit. Yes, his family name was marred already, because of what his brother did. He had a target placed on him forever. She could understand his reasoning. His brother's disregard for human life started it all. This was his way of trying to stop the rippling effect of ruin from growing any larger.

"Sy …"

"Shut up! Nothin' you say, is gonna change my mind. If you don't wanna die, you'll keep your fucking mouth shut. I don't wanna hear no more."

She raised her palms in supplication.

"Okay. I understand and I'm sorry that you're going through this." She lowered her palms and placed her right hand over her heart, in hopes of getting him to calm down, and believe her. "Your boss was wrong to judge you so harshly. It wasn't fair. It was so unjust. I'll help all I can."

He stared her down, and she noticed his breathing calming. All she could do now, was try and win maybe his trust. Try and get him to believe, that she was on his side. She tried to remember to talk to him in soft tones, use his first name often, and get him talking on subjects that didn't make him angry. He directed his gaze towards the boy and pointed to the sack, barking out commands.

"Tape her mouth, tie her wrists behind her back, and cuff her ankles. We're the fuck outta here."

Jessica decided not to struggle and simply stood still. She smiled tenderly, when the boy stepped forward and mouthed 'sorry.'

She would not give up hope, she thought silently. Time was still on her side, and she knew that being a lot more cunning and smarter, was also as well.

CHAPTER NINETEEN

Bryan stormed from his office, with a look that told his staff, he was a man on a mission and enraged.

Claire was in the middle of conversing with Missy, and Zachary, as his office door flew open, taking them all by surprise.

"Did you hear from her? Has Jessica called in at all?"

Heads shook fervently in response, and he did not wait for them to verbalize their thoughts either. He stormed to the back office, finding Connor's door open.

"She's not here! Something's wrong. I just know it." He pulled out his cell phone and showed Connor her last text message.

Connor read it quickly and popped up out of his chair. "That was thirty minutes ago. She should be back by now."

Bryan turned and found the rest of his staff there, standing in wait of instructions, fear clearly mirrored upon their faces. He raised his hand for pause, as he depressed the green phone icon next to Ayden's name.

"Hey –"Ayden said, before being cut off.

Bryan's voice was curt and fearful. "She's missing. Tell me you found something."

"I'm waiting on a fax as we speak. I managed to get the tapes. After running through the first ten minutes of the first three days of the trial, he appears in every one of them."

"God damn it," Bryan snapped.

"Bry, look. I'll find out his name in the next few minutes. All felon cases tried at the courthouse now, mandates that all court visitors sign in and show a photo idea, which is scanned into the system. I've got them pulling day one from the archives and faxing them a.s.a.p. We'll have a name to match the face right away. Be patient, Bry. I'm 90% percent certain he needs her. She's safe for now."

"It's the other 10% that worries me." Bryan replied and disconnected the line.

He looked at his office manager and gave an order. "Claire, I have a photo on my desk I need you to show to the guide, who headed the Capitol tour, Jessica was on today that started at noon. See, if she recognizes the man in the photo. Also, get a list from here of the names of the people, who participated in that tour."

Claire moved swiftly into Bryan's office, found a picture on his desk and returned.

"Is this the one, Senator?"

He nodded and she was out of the office doing his bidding quickly.

"Whoever did this, Senator, probably wasn't stupid enough to sign up for that tour."

Connor interrupted.

"I know, but it's good to check everything off. More than likely, he followed her from a distance, and caught her unawares up on the sixth floor. If only …"

He shook his head in dismay. 'If onlys', didn't matter right now. Her curiosity wasn't at fault here. The madman, who chose to abduct her was, and he had to get on his trail, while it was still hot.

He looked at the faces of his staff, still milling around him, waiting for some direction. He ran his fingers through his hair and sighed, as though the weight of the world was just placed upon his shoulders.

Connor came up beside him, clasping his shoulder firmly to let him know they would all work through this together.

Bryan directed his staff calmly.

"I have reason to believe that the man, who attempted to accost Jessica on her first day, did so this afternoon, shortly after her tour of the Capitol came to an end." The look of horror on their faces and gasps of dismay, made tears prickle behind his eyes. "We have some strong, solid leads, as to who this guy is. I'm waiting to hear from my former partner at Albany PD in the next few minutes, as to our next move.

I know you're all as concerned and worried as I am. We'll get through this together. If I hear anything positive, I promise you all will be the first to know."

He nodded toward his office for Connor to follow him, and then closed the door behind them, when he entered. Right then his cell phone rang, and he recognized Ayden's number. He depressed the button for speaker, so Connor could hear as well.

"Speak to me, bro."

"Good news, Bry. That guy in the photo, is Sylas Corbat."

"Corbat! Is he related to that wacko, who gunned down Michaelson's son?"

"The one and the same. He was in that courtroom every day, Bry."

"So, I was right. It is a vendetta and has something to do with his brother being sentenced and my bill."

Missy pushed opened his office door so hard, it slammed against the wall. The doorknob left a depression in the wall. Bryan and Connor jumped from the unexpected interruption. The look of horror marring her delicate features told him contact had been made. Her voice shook with fear as she blurted out. "Senator, a man … a man is on the phone. He says he has Jessica and wants to talk to you."

Bryan closed the distance between them and placed his palm tenderly against his receptionist's cheek.

"It's okay, Missy. Put the call through."
She nodded nervously and quickly darted back
to her desk.

"Keep our call open, Bry, and hit the record
button on your cell." Ayden's voice instructed.

"K," Bryan replied and did as Ayden
suggested, just as his office line rang.

His cheeks puffed as he blew out a deep
breath, looked at Connor, and picked up the
receiver on the second ring.

"Tell me what you want." He ordered.

"Barking orders already, Senator? I'm the
one in control right now." Sylas sardonically
replied.

"You don't need to harm her, Corbat. Why
don't you just let her go, before you get
yourself in any deeper. I'll do whatever you
ask."

"Smart man, I see. I want the bill killed.
Whatever you need to do, to make it go away.

She stays with me, until I hear on the news it's done."

"Corbat, this bill has been argued by those before me for years. Even, if I did what you asked, which I can and will, should I leave office right after that … whoever takes my place, will, could, might pick up the cause and bring it back to life again. This is senseless. Please."

"Yah, well, my fucking name is dirt! I got fired. The news is calling this the Corbat Death Penalty Bill. Would you want that noose around your neck the rest of your fucking life? Kill the fucking bill, find a way to keep it dead, or I kill your bitch. Plain and simple."

The dial tone buzzed in his ear and Bryan hung up.

"There's no getting through to him, Bryan." Connor exclaimed. "He's fixated on one thing … the bill not becoming law <u>ever</u>."

"The only way that'll happen is, if the Supreme Court deems it unconstitutional. You know, and I know, that's not going to happen. There's been strong arguments in our favor it no longer violates the 8th Amendment prohibiting against cruel and unusual punishment. No one is using hanging, beheading, or electrocution anymore. With lethal injections, those bastards fall to a peaceful death. Far from what they deserve."

"Can't you get one of those black cloaks to make a bogus announcement it's been found unconstitutional in New York?" Ayden piped in.

"Good ploy, Ayden, but not in this lifetime."

"So, we find him our way. We've done it countless times. You can still tell him you'll need to reach out to each of the Justice's to consider your request, and it will take a little while. In the meantime, you'll hold the bill up in your committee."

"It's the only choice we have right now." Bryan agreed.

"I'll pin down where this guy lives. Who his friends are? Where he worked, and we'll go from there?"

"Thanks, Ayden."

"You welcome, bro. And, Bry … the Captain put me on this case. You know he hates the Feds and Troopers gaining glory in his precinct. I'm on this 24/7."

Bryan chuckled lightly. It was comforting to know that one of the best detectives on the force, minus himself, of course, was on the case. If anyone could help him find Jessica, Ayden Tyler could. He was hopeful.

"Talk to you soon," he ended.

CHAPTER TWENTY

Her abductor was smarter, than she had given him credit for. She had hoped they would keep her hidden up on the sixth floor, so Bryan could find her eventually. That was not the case. As soon as they gagged her and tied her arms and cuffed her legs, they pulled a flat hand truck on wheels from around the corner with a long, black sack on top of it.

She wasn't stupid. She knew they would put her in the sack and roll her out of here in the light of day. She'd go kicking and screaming, if she had too. That decision, however, was taken away from her.

Sy pulled two grey jumpsuits from the bag that had the word U-Haul embroidered on the back of them. The two men stepped into the jumpsuits and zipped them up. Sy pulled a small vial from the breast pocket of his, poured the liquid contents onto a cloth, and approached her with a devilish look upon his face.

"Time for you to go nighty night, princess." He laughed heartily.

Before she could react, the cloth was pressed to her nose and darkness overcame her.

Jessica awoke, bleary-eyed and with a rhythmic, heavy pounding against her temples, that made her moan aloud. She felt dizzy and groggy, and knew she could fall back asleep, if she wanted to. She remembered she was in danger and forced her mind to focus on the here and now.

She remembered being abducted, tied up and gagged. She couldn't feel her fingers, as her bindings were tight enough to cut off her circulation. It took her a few moments to maneuver them, so she could sit up, and push herself against a solid rock wall with her feet. The surface felt cold against her back, and with her fingers, she could feel in some places it was as smooth as glass, and in others, jagged.

It took a moment for her eyes to adjust to the darkness that engulfed her. She could hear the constant drip, drip, dripping of water falling into a puddle. The sound echoed and it wasn't hard to figure out that she was inside some kind of cave.

Despite it was nearly November, the temperature inside was amazingly comfortable. If she had to guess, it might have been around fifty degrees, maybe more. Her wool slacks helped to keep her comfortable, as did her matching suit coat and the lightly-knitted scooped-neck sweater she wore underneath. When she felt, a steady cool breeze blowing in from somewhere to her right, it ruffled her long hair and made her skin prickle.

"Where in god's name did he bring me?" She wondered.

A strip of tape had been plastered over her mouth to keep her from calling out. She could feel her bag was still strapped across her chest and the familiarity of it gave her some sense of comfort.

She knew she wasn't alone. The quick chips of noise she heard overhead along with the flapping of wings, told her the cave was occupied by a colony of bats. It didn't much bother her, because she knew they were known not to attack humans.

She wondered how long she had been out cold. All she could remember, was how sweet the liquid smelled, when the man named Sy Corbat, pressed the cloth against her nose and mouth. Almost immediately, her legs and arms went numb, her vision blurred, and her hearing faded. Then, puff, that was it. She didn't remember anything else.

She tested the bounds around her wrists, again. There was no give at all, and she moaned from the pain the movement created. There was no way she would be able to work the knot free, unless that is, if she kept rubbing the rope up against the jagged rocks behind her

Maybe, I can strip it away enough to snap it.

Jessica wasn't going to just sit there. She knew that. As much as she believed that Bryan, would find her, she couldn't sit idle and wait. She had to make good her escape, before Corbat decided she was no longer of any use to him. First though, she would wait a while. She knew that her captors most assuredly, would come and check on her.

Jessica prayed that it would be the young man, instead of Corbat. She knew she could talk and sway him to her side. It was plainly obvious, the young man wanted nothing to do with kidnapping her. Corbat was a bully, and the poor kid was fearful of him. She was too. She couldn't let her fear consume and disable her and stop her from getting the hell out of here. She also couldn't believe this was happening to her. She would lose it, if she had to stay in here too long in the darkness. God only knows, what kind of animals and insects made their home in here. Suddenly, she felt itchy and screamed inside her head.

"Stop it!"

She couldn't let her mind, play such stupid tricks on her. No, she didn't want to be in here. Yes, she wanted to be back at her office. But, as luck had it, she was someone's prisoner. She had to stay strong and figure out a way to get the hell out of here. She had to make this work to her advantage.

She didn't have to wait long. She heard someone entering, before she saw a soft glow of light emitting from either a lantern or flashlight. She could tell from the person's silhouette it was the tall, thin boy.

She started to moan loudly over-and-over again. He had to remove the taping from her mouth. He just had too. She tried desperately to raise up on her knees. Jagged stones dug through the fabric of her slacks, but she did not care. She crawled forward on her knees, her eyes pleading with him to remove the tape, as she continued to moan.

The look of sympathy that shone in his eyes told her, that he was weakening, and she continued her plea, this time whimpering.

The young man knelt before her, placed the two lanterns he was carrying down on the ground beside him.

"Don't fret now. Stop squirming. This may hurt a little cause I'm gonna pull it off real fast."

She nodded that she understood.

He was right. It hurt like hell, and she yelped loudly, as the tape ripped at her tender skin, making it sting. It felt as though he grated a worn razor over the entire area instead.

"Sorry. Shit, I'm sorry!"

She tried to work her way into a sitting position, but she lost her balance and fell to her side, slamming her right cheek against a boulder nearby. She cried out in pain and the young man moved like a bullet to help her sit upright.

"Damn! This ain't workin' out too good."

She knew the gash was deep and could feel a stream of warm blood running down her cheek

Shit! Piss! Tits! That hurt! Her inner voice screamed.

"I'm … I'm just glad it's you," she gasped, "and not that mad man Corbat here right now." She replied, gasping loudly again, as she leaned against the boulder.

"Why's that?" He asked surprisingly.

"Because, I knew right away, when I first saw you, that you weren't the kind of person to hurt someone, and I was right?" She shrugged her right shoulder, so she could rub her cheek against it and wipe away the blood she could feel flowing down her cheek.

He nodded shyly and lifted one of the lanterns, so he could look at her wound closer. He grimaced at what he saw.

"You hit yourself real bad, mam. I'll getcha a Band-Aid and ointment, when I go back up top."

"Jessica. Call me, Jessica. Will you leave one of them here for me? Please." She nodded toward the other lantern on her right. "It's a little frightful down here alone in the darkness."

He nodded, that he would, and avoided looking at her.

"What's your name?"

"Morris,' he replied in a soft whisper. He chewed at his lip and his voice broke with emotion. "I didn't want to do this."

The fear on his face tugged at her heartstrings again and she answered him in a soothing tone.

"I know, Morris. I could tell that right away too, about you. Did you and he work together down here?"

"Ah, ha," he answered.

Jessica knew she had to keep the conversation going. The more she got him to open up to her, the more comfortable, she knew he would feel around her. He was an innocent. She didn't think he was a simpleton. She had a feeling he didn't finish high school, but had enough good sense to know right from wrong.

"How long?"

"Been down here, since I was eighteen. Didn't graduate from high school. Too hard for me, but Mr. Howe, he knew my grandpa and hired me right off. He was the best boss ever, real kind, and all." He paused a moment, and a deep sadness washed over him. "He died though, and someone else bought these caves. He's a mean son of bitch." The boy's head popped up, realizing a cuss word slipped from his lips. "Sorry, mam. Didn't mean to say swear words, but he's a cruel man, just like Sy."

"Where is Sy now?"

"He ain't here, but he'll be back later tonight. He knows how to get underground, even when it's all locked up top."

"Does the owner know he can do that?"

He shook his head no in response.

"Morris, did Sy threaten and beat you into doing this."

She could tell she hit the nail on the head by the boy's reaction. The poor kid. She wondered about his family, if he was totally alone in the world, or whether someone knew he was being bullied.

"Morris, did he?" She persisted.

The boy ran his hand through his dirty hair and hesitated another moment, before he finally answered.

"He told me … that … that …if'n I didn't help; he'd blow up these caves with me in it, when I less expected it. He'll do it too. I need this job and gots nowhere else to go."

"Morris, what if I could help you? You know I work for a State Senator. He's a very important man, and my Aunt, is a very rich woman, who knows a lot of people in power. You like to fix things, don't you Morris?"

A slow knowing smile lit up his face, despite the smeared dirt, and what looked like oil all over it and the clothes he wore too.

"I'm real good, mam, with my hands." He raised them. "I can do and fix just about anything somebody asks me too. I can use a

digger and a backhoe and a jack hammer too."
He answered proudly, as he thumbed his chest
to prove his point.

"Well, I think that's pretty, darn awesome. I
know I could help you find a job doing just
that, working for someone, who would
appreciate the fine work you do for them. The
people we know would pay you a good salary,
offer you great benefits, and treat you with
respect and kindness. Isn't that something you
would like? You deserve it you know."

He scratched at his head, and it began to
slowly shake with doubt.

"I don't know, mam. If Sy ever found out
we was talking like this, he wouldn't take too
kind to that."

"Well, I won't tell him." She confirmed
immediately. "It can be our little secret. When
someone mean like Sy bully's a person like you
to do his bidding, the law will understand

especially, if I tell them, you helped me, took care of me, and kept me from harm."

"You would do that for me?" His eyes misted with tears. He wiped at them quickly, so she wouldn't see, but she did.

"Yes, Morris. I would do that for you, if you helped me get away. I promise, I will stand up for you in court, and help you get a better job too."

He started to get all fidgety and unable to contain his discomfort.

"I really got to think about all this. Sure, sounds too good to be true."

"Okay. Okay. We have time." She waited a moment and tried to get in a more comfortable position. It was difficult. "Morris, can you tie my hands in front of me instead? My arms hurt, and I can't feel my hands. It's so uncomfortable this way. My legs are cuffed. I can't go anywhere with them like this. Please, just my hands. Will you do that for me." She made a great effort to look forlorn, and it worked.

"Ah, gee, I don't know, miss. If you get away, he'll -"

She pressed harder. "Not like this, I won't." She demonstrated, trying to move her legs, and attempting to stand. When she toppled forward, he reached out to catch her.

"Stop that now, before you hurt yourself again. Okay. I will."

He paused momentarily, as if an afterthought, had him second guessing his decision. His forehead crunched with worry and his lips pressed tightly together. He nodded curtly and stepped forward and moved behind her, careful not to tug too hard on her bindings.

When her wrists were free, she cried out in pain, as her arms dropped to her side like heavy weights. She sat there for a moment, her arms still lifeless at her side, letting the blood slowly recirculate through her veins. The pain was excruciating, and she couldn't stop the flow of tears.

Morris, fell to his knees and looked terribly regretful.

"Gee, miss. Don't cry. I sure didn't mean to hurt ya."

Slowly, she managed to move her arms, and began to massage them with her hands to help get the blood moving faster. They throbbed painfully and she did her best to try and stop from crying. She hated getting her wrists tied again, but she knew she had too. If anything, this time, she'd be able to manage getting at the contents in her bag a lot easier.

"It's okay, Morris. The pain is subsiding now. It's just because the rope was too tight and stopped the blood flowing up and down my arm.:

"I told him he tied it too tight. He don't listen to no one, but the monster inside his head."

It was a great analogy he made. Morris wasn't as dim-witted as he thought of himself. He was insightful and caring … good qualities to be proud of. She raised her arms and crossed her wrists in front of him.

"Go ahead. I'll be okay. I enjoyed talking to you, and I thank you for the lantern," she nodded at the element to her right. "How long will the battery last?"

The boy smiled proudly. "I just put a fresh one in for ya. It's a good one too, and will last more than a week, if you keep it turned down low like that."

She expelled a breath loudly.

"Well, my friend. Hopefully, I won't be in here that long."

Her stomach growled loudly, and the sound bounced off the cave walls and echoed throughout the chamber. She gazed up at him and chuckled, and before she knew it, he was laughing as well.

She snorted and remarked.

"Guess I'm a little hungry."

"There's some leftover donuts up in the lounge room where we take our breaks. I'll go get you a few and a bottle of water too, and fix your cut." He rose, picked up the second lantern and started to walk away.

"Thank you," she called out to him.

"You welcome, mam," he replied politely. "I'll be back in about forty minutes or so, by the time I get up top and return."

"I'll be here when you get back," she answered, and heard him chuckle softly, as though her reply tickled his funny bone.

Knowing she had forty minutes, before he returned, Jessica tried to work her hands into her shoulder bag. There was something to be said for women, who carried bags the size of a small attaché. She had everything, but the kitchen sink inside hers. It was her bag on the go. As her fingertips grazed along the inside, she could feel her small mist bottle of breath freshener, a packet of matches, chewing gum, two tissue packs, a protein bar she forgot about, her change purse, wallet, key chain, cell phone, and yes, her gun.

She pulled her cell out first. She knew she wouldn't be able to get a signal this far below the ground. She knew Bryan was smart enough to check the ping on her phone. After the last time, she was attacked, security had downloaded a GPS tracker to her phone. She prayed, that the signal would work in this godforsaken cave. She checked the app to make sure it was active, and smiled when she noted, that the green indicator button was in the on position.

She placed it on a silent mode, and put it on the ground beside her. Next, she removed her gun from her bag as well. She did not want Corbat to find either one of them, in case he eventually checked her bag. She was rather surprised he hadn't already. Sometimes when someone, was in a fit of rage, they lost sight of the obvious, and thankfully it worked in her favor. She reached out for the lantern and held it out in front of her. Carefully, she checked around her for a good place to hide her phone and gun, yet close enough to reach it, in case she ever needed it.

There, less than six inches to her right, was a crevice between the boulder she fell against and another one right beside it. It was big enough for just that purpose. When she raised the lantern in all directions, the shadows reflecting off the boulders, hid the crevice even better. She was rather pleased with herself and huffed with satisfaction, as she slid both items inside.

She lifted her hand to her cheek. It was, extremely tender to the touch, and there was a pretty good-sized bump developing. She shimmied away from the boulder and slowly let her eyes scan her surroundings. She sighed with disbelief. She couldn't believe, where she was right now.

The chamber she was in, was massive. When she looked up, she couldn't see the roof of the cave at all. The walls shimmered, where the beam from the lantern managed to reach. Despite the eeriness, she found herself rather awe-struck by its natural beauty.

She didn't know much about caves. What she had learned and read about, was that some were formed when water seeped down through the cracks in limestone rock over millions of years. Others, simply were mountainsides worn away by the crashing ocean waves over time.

It was hard to tell, from where she was sitting, if the glimmering reflections she was seeing, were from crystals on the walls. The other formations, she was looking at, were rather hard to describe. Still, they were uniquely beautiful. They were swirled, and rippled, spiked, and textured, massive pieces the colors of an earth-tone pallet. The enormity of the chamber was not threatening, but she knew that silence for too long of time, would prove oppressive.

She drew her knees to her chest, managed to fold her bounded wrists over them, and rested her undamaged cheek on her knees. The thought of her Aunt Florence came to mind. As much as she would love nothing more, than to have her there by her side, she wouldn't wish this situation she now found herself in on anyone, not even her worst enemy. Well ... one bastard did come to mind.

If Florence had the chance to get a message to her, Jessica knew, that her Aunt would tell her to stay strong, not to crack, keep a smart head on her shoulders, and work every situation to her advantage.

That wasn't going to be easy in this case ... at all.

Her stomach growled again, and she thought about her protein bar. She tried to ignore the sound of starvation. Morris would be returning soon. She had to conserve it for later, just in case Corbat decided to be a prick and starve her.

She would wait for Morris, as the satisfaction in knowing, that she made a friend in him, kept her company, until he did.

CHAPTER TWENTY-ONE

Bryan left word with his staff, that if Sylas Corbat called for him, to direct him to his cell phone. He just couldn't sit around in his office waiting for that derelict to call. The clock was ticking. He had worked enough kidnap cases to know that the first twenty-four hours were crucial. It wasn't a lot of time for him and Ayden to turn over every stone possible and investigate every lead. They zoned in on the ones that were most likely.

The one thing in their favor … they knew who the assailant was. Protocol was, to call in the Feds in situations like this. He wanted it contained. He wanted to run this case. He wanted to be the one to find her, and he would.

Ayden pulled up in front of the LOB and Bryan quickly jumped into the passenger side.

"Thanks for doing this. I just can't sit around."

"Good to have you back, partner," Ayden winked.

Bryan sent him that 'how did you know' look, and Ayden's stomach rolled with laughter.

"I know you, man. It's pretty god damn obvious. You found the one."

Bryan's look was more serious, as he replied painfully.

"We've got to get her back."

Ayden punched at his forearm, nodding and replied sympathetically.

"We will, Bry. We will." He hesitated only briefly. "This prick, Corbat, lives in a decent neighborhood up in Esperance. There's four to his apartment house. I checked around and scuttlebutt is, no one has seen him in days.

One of the guys in his building knew what he was driving. It's an old 64 Chevy Corvair Greenbrier van, two-tone light blue in color. The thing is a classic, so it stands out. More than likely, it's what he used to transport her in. It's possible he's living out of it too, because back then, they were manufactured as mini-campers on wheels.

I ran footage from the security cameras outside your building, and we got a hit. One was seen exiting the back entrance of the Capitol around the time Jessica was missing, heading west on State Street. Looks like he's got an accomplice too. A traffic camera picked up two male occupants, and one of them, was definitely Corbat. They're running a facial on the other one. They were last scene, heading North on the Interstate, where we lost them."

"At least we've got something solid to go on," Bryan replied. "I called my contact at the DA's office. They had info. on next of kin.

Looks like Luther's brother had been working at Howes Caverns as an all-round handyman for years, which backs up his story. If he's been fired though, he won't have access any more. I still think it's worth checking out."

Ayden nodded in agreement.

"Just because he's fired, doesn't mean he still hasn't got a way inside, especially after all those years he's been there. Sounds like a great hideout to me."

Bryan keyed in the address on the dashboard GPS system.

"This is a sweet ride. What is it a 15'?"

"Yep. I confiscated it in a drug raid a month ago. This baby went for $85K brand new and has all the bells and whistles."

"It'll be great, if ever you're in pursuit off-road."

"Can't wait to test and see what she's made of."

Bryan's cell rang and he answered it immediately, when he recognized Connor's phone number flashing on the screen.

"Hey, Connor, what's up?"

"I just wanted to let you know the Clerk's office is holding the bill. It won't be going up for a vote before both Houses, until we give them the go ahead. I leaked it to the news, and the major networks will run it, as will the three radio stations. Whatever Corbat listens to, or watches, he'll at least know you're trying to work with him."

"Awesome, Connor. Thanks. I'm incognito, buddy for the rest of the week. Clair's clearing my calendar, as we speak."

"I know. I got your message. If anyone can find Jessica, Bry. You two cowboys can."

Bryan chuckled at the jibe. "Feels good to be back in the saddle again. Wish me luck."

"You don't need it," Connor replied confidently. "I've seen you in your badass mode before. Fucking get that guy and bring our girl back!"

"I plan on it. I'll check in later."

Bryan shared what Connor just told him.

"All the stations have been notified that the bill's been removed from both houses for a vote. At least, Corbat will know I'm cooperating, and it'll give us some time to find Jessica."

"That's good news."

"Did you ping her phone." Bryan asked.

Ayden nodded his reply.

"We lost her signal an hour after she texted you last. Could be because she's out of range, or her battery was low."

"I'm waiting to hear back from security. I talked to them just before you picked me up. It's mandatory now, that all the members have a Follow Me app downloaded onto their phones, in case of situations like this. I had the app added to Jessica's phone, after Corbat's attempt the first time. It has a stealth mode on it too, that hides the app icon on the screen."

Bryan's cell phone rang again. The caller ID indicated unknown, but he pressed the button just in case it was Corbat.

"Bryan Gallagher here."

"Smart thing you listened," Corbat said on the other end of the line. "You better keep the fucking cops off my trail too, or she's dead. You got it?"

Bryan depressed the speaker button right away as he signaled Ayden it was Corbat on the other end of the line.

"I want to speak with her?"

"No. Ain't with her. Besides, I've come up with a better plan. I did a little checking on your girlfriend, Senator. She's a rich one, and, a m-i-g-h-t-y, rich one, at that. You want her back safe and alive, then, scramble up …oh … let's say … two million in one-hundred-dollar bills by tomorrow night, and she's all yours."

"It won't be a problem, but I'm not making any calls to get the ball rolling, until I talk to her first!"

There was a moment of silent contemplation. Bryan knew getting the cash wouldn't be a problem. Florence probably had that amount sitting in a locked safe at home, or a safety box at her primary bank. He had to make sure, that Jessica was unharmed. He needed to let her know, that he was coming for her.

Corbat's tone was curt, but at least, he complied.

"Alright. Not until tonight, when I go check on her. I'll call you at eleven."

"I expected that," Bryan remarked, after the line was disconnected.

"Yah, me too. At least it gives us another twenty-four hours to find her first."

It took them nearly forty minutes to drive up to the popular tourist attraction known as Howe Caverns. It was an impressive spot with its gigantic white letters spelled out on the front lawn. They saw the lettering first, before the huge building came into view.

"I've heard about this place, but never been here. How about you?"

"Came with my seventh-grade class. It's really awesome inside with its underground caves and lake."

A chill ran up and down Bryan's spine. All he could think of was Jessica, tied up like an animal in a dark, dank cave all alone. This was the perfect place to keep her too, and why wouldn't he. Corbat worked here for years. He probably knew every inch of the caves and where to hide her. Management wouldn't be the wiser. Bryan knew she wouldn't be in the most likely places though, particularly not where the tours were conducted.

He had her in an area that either, hadn't been discovered yet, or decided on not making accessible to the public for monetary reasons. They had less than twenty-four hours to find her, and he prayed, they found the right place.

As they began to walk towards the main building, Bryan's phone rang again, and he recognized the main number for the Capitol Police.

"Bryan here."

"Senator it's Sgt. Taft."

"Mac, been waiting on your call. Tell me you've got something."

"You're there already."

"What? She's here at Howe Caverns."

"I knew you wouldn't sit idle. The cop in you wouldn't allow it. Both of your signals are coming from there right now. You want back up? I can call the greys in. They've got a sub-station right there in Schoharie."

"No. No, Mac. I don't want to scare him off. We've got to move slow on this one. Thanks, a million. If her signal changes, even minutely, text me. Once we go in, we'll go silent."

"My eyes are glued to the screen, until you bring her home, Senator. If you change your mind about backup, call me."

"Will do."

He directed his attention to Ayden.

"You heard?"

Ayden nodded, smiling and asked. "You wanna do the questioning? This guy may recognize you."

Bryan shook his head no and responded. "At this point I don't care. I'm along for the ride. You take the lead on this one."

The moment they entered, it was plainly clear the place might have been closed for reconstruction. Scaffolds were off to the right and the front lobby desk and furniture was covered with paint drop cloths.

"Can any one of you point me to the office?" Ayden called out to the workers, who turned when they entered the building.

The painter closest to them acknowledged first, pointing off to the left.

"Take that corridor to the left. First office on your right."

Bryan and Ayden both nodded their thanks and went in the direction given.

The front office was empty, but they noticed a balding, rotund male in the office in the rear and headed that way.

"We're closed," he barked out, noticing their approach.

Ayden unsnapped his badge and made it visible.

"Det. Ayden Tyler, Albany P.D. I've got a few questions, if you don't mind. You the owner?"

The owner huffed his disgust as he picked up a burning stogy from the ash tray on his desk and took a puff. He scrutinized them both, turned his back to them, and plopped down into his chair behind the desk.

"It's about fucking Corbat, isn't it?"

"When did you last see him?" Ayden pursued.

"Two days ago, when I let him go. I had to, because of that waste of a brother of his. Couldn't have him around anymore. If the press got hold he worked here, it would've been bad for business. You understand."

"Quite frankly, no I don't. He's not responsible for what his brother did." Ayden reprimanded.

"Fuck you. I can fire whoever I want."

Ayden moved fast, closing the distance between them

"Well, asshole," Ayden spat, as he leaned over him with a look of intimidation, that made the owner swallow nervously, "you pushed him over the edge … enough so, he kidnapped a woman, and it's more than likely he's got her held up here."

"Christ. I don't need this shit. Not now. I'm supposed to open soon."

"Well, you are fucked, unless you cooperate."

The owner thought briefly and sent him a questioning look before answering.

"Yah, just how do you figure that?"

Bryan stepped in and answered for Ayden.

"Look. He knows your closed for business obviously. It's our assumption he doesn't have her in an area where your workers are, where sightseers would normally venture. He's worked these caves long enough; he knows them better than anyone. There's got to be chambers, once discovered and not open to the public. Do you have any idea where they might be?"

The owner nodded and then leaned to his right and slid the bottom drawer open of his desk. He pulled out a large-folded paper that resembled a map and spread it open across his desk.

"There's two chambers I'm aware of. Here and here," he pointed. "They're pretty accessible, if your dressed for it. "He looked up at them both and waved his hand, "not like that though. You need to come back in jeans, sweatshirt, or sweater maybe, and work boots. Floors are jagged and dangerous down there."

"Is this map clear enough for someone like us to follow."

"Yah. I had no trouble. This point begins right off the elevator," he indicated the spot on the map. "Only one way down, I know of. He may have an exit point from outside I don't know about too. He was a sneaky bastard. Like you said, he's been here long enough. Could be another chamber too, and not one of these? There's nearly two miles of cave below ground."

"I'll take that, if you don't mind?" Ayden directed.

The owner rolled up the map and handed it to him. He pulled a set of keys from the top drawer and handed those over as well.

"These will open the front door. Workers will be out of here by five. In the front office is a cabinet, where you'll find headlamps, lanterns, and flashlights. Use what you need."

Bryan replied. "We'll wait until dark. Thanks for your cooperation, and please, not a word to anyone."

The owner stared at him for a moment longer than needed.

"Hey, ain't you that Senator, whose been on the news so much?"

Bryan acknowledged with a nod.

"So, what's your interest in all this?" The owner pressed.

"The woman he kidnapped, is a member of my staff."

CHAPTER TWENTY-TWO

The waitress, who looked like she'd been ridden hard, shuffled to their table like it pained her to move. She set two cups of steaming, hot coffee down on the table with arthritic hands.

Sy waved her off, when she politely asked, if they wanted to order something to eat. His brusqueness certainly did not bother her any as she remarked, "Suit yourself, sonny. Makes no never mind to me."

His coffee companion chortled at the woman's response and blew at the hot liquid to cool it down, before taking a sip.

Sy looked around to see if anyone conspicuous was paying too much attention to them both and was satisfied things appeared to be normal. He chose this old diner for a good reason. It was way out in East bejesus, and not a likely place where anyone would know him. There were a few late morning stragglers sucking down coffee. They looked like local farmers and delivery folk passing through.

"You hiding her, where you said?"

"You think I'm lying?" Sy snarled in reply.

"Don't get your underwear all twisted, Corbat." His associate snapped. "There better not be a mark on her."

Sy didn't like this prick ... not one bit. He hated that he refused to tell Sy his name. He understood why though. Couldn't rat out someone, if you didn't know their name. He could give a flying fuck, if his was Tinkerbell. The guy was smooth as butter. He knew how to cover his ass. He probably made a living out of fucking people over his entire life.

The bastard didn't mind paying him two million to get what he wanted either. He didn't even blink, when Sy asked for it. He wanted the woman bad.

Sy still couldn't believe his luck, when the guy first approached him outside the courtroom, after his brother was found guilty. Funny thing though, Sy never noticed him at the Courthouse one time, during the entire trial. He had to have someone sit in for him, tell him what was going on every day, and who was there. How else would he have known?

Didn't matter any. He was getting what he asked for. Now, that he switched the plan to suit his fancy, and collecting another two mill from the Senator, he was gonna be set for life.

"There you go doubting me again. I told ya, how many times now, everything went off without a hitch? She's being watched. No one knows she's there. I called Gallagher back at eleven like I said I would and let him talk to her. If you came in yesterday, you would have had her by now and I'd be the fuck out of here. She's yours tonight like <u>you</u> planned so, chill the hell out."

The man snickered, pleased as punch, that his plan was playing out nicely.

"For a smart man, Gallagher certainly fell for the bullshit you fed him."

Sy shrugged, as he looked at the guy across from him and replied nonchalantly. "I can be real convincing, when I want too."

This guy was one shrewd bastard. He talked kind of funny, but Sy knew he could afford just about anything from the way he dressed and the car he rented out in the parking lot. If the diamond on his pinky finger was any larger, the fucker wouldn't be able to raise it high enough to pick the buggers from his nose. Thinking about it made him snicker.

"You want to share what's so funny?"

"Just the fact the almighty Senator thinks I did all this, because of my fucking brother. That prick Tallon firing me, just made the story sweeter and more convincing."

"And the Caverns are still on lock down?"

Sy tested his coffee to see, if it had cooled enough to take a sip. It was, and he sucked down two, long gulps, before answering.

"Renovations will be going on for another two weeks, before they can open. Workers are all gone by five. I'll have her up top after ten, just to make sure. She'll be in room two-eighteen, tied and spread out for ya. What you do with her, after I'm paid and gone, I could give a shit. Just make sure you got my cash as agreed."

His associate took a money clip from his pant pocket.

Sy nearly gasped from its thickness, as the guy thumbed through hundreds and twenties, until he pulled a ten-dollar bill from the wad and threw it down on the table.

He scooted back his chair, stood, and gazed down at him and directed with authority, before stepping away, "Don't keep me waiting. Ten o'clock, and not a second later."

Sy took his time finishing his coffee and exited the diner, as he called Morris on his cell.

"Ya," the kid answered nervously.

"You feed her?"

"Just now. Boss was real pissed about something. Said not to come back in, until tomorrow. I don't like this. It ain't right."

"Don't matter what you like, or don't like, boy. Keep your mouth shut, and do as I say, or you die. Plain and simple. Besides, I don't need you, no more. She'll be gone tonight."

The kid hesitated a moment, before he pressed on. "Can't leave her down there all day without checking on her. What if some'thin happens ta her?"

"Ain't nothing gonna happen," Sy blared, losing his patience. "She's been fine all along, hasn't she? She's got the lantern. She's been fed. I'll be getting her out of there by ten." He disconnected the line without further argument and entered his car to leave.

CHAPTER TWENTY-THREE

Jessica hated the way she smelled. She wanted nothing more than to soak in a bubble bath, until her skin pruned up. If it wasn't for the two packets of tissues she had in her bag, she'd be smelling worse from squatting and relieving herself down here. Even, that smell, was getting to her. As much as she tried to find an area far enough from where she sat and slept, it didn't prove far away enough.

She wanted to punch Corbat square in the month when he came to visit her last night. She hadn't seen him since her abduction. He never told her, why he was removing the cuffs from her ankles. All he did was keep poking her back, and pushing her forward along a thin path she didn't know even existed, that led out of the chamber she was kept in. Her legs were weak, and she had a hard time standing, let alone walking. Every time she fell, he dragged her by the collar of her suit coat.

God! How she hated the son of a bitch. If only her hands were free. If only the circulation in her limbs hadn't been cut off for so long, she could have disabled him.

It wasn't until they were in cell range, that the reason for her tortuous journey above ground made sense. Hearing Bryan's voice made it all worthwhile. His voice was like a caress. It gave her hope. It made her believe in the possibility of seeing the light of day once more. That's all she thought about on her trip back down into darkness.

Once Corbat left her, she couldn't stop crying about the ever-expectant joy of seeing Bryan again, holding him, kissing him, and telling him how much she had fallen in love with him. Hearing his voice, had given her renewed hope. There was something in the tone of it though, something in what he said, that made her believe, the signal on her phone had worked and he knew where she was.

What was it? She wracked her brain to try and remember.

Their conversation had been brief. It hadn't lasted any more than two minutes, at the most. She thought for a moment, trying to think back, as to what he had said to her … how he said it … how adamant he was.

Corbat wasn't a stupid man. He warned Bryan he had him on speaker and she knew Bryan would play it smart and be careful with the exchange between he and her.

The first words he had spoken, made her cry though. She didn't want to. She wanted him to know she was strong. She couldn't help it, when the tears started to flow, and her voice cracked with emotion.

"You okay, honey?"

"Bryan, oh god, Bryan!"

"It's all going to work out, babe. Just stay calm. I've got you. Do you hear me, Jessica? I've got you."

She wanted to say more, tell him she loved him. But Corbat had pulled the cell away from her ear. She wanted to kick out at him, but didn't have the strength, when he began to mimic, what Bryan had said to her. The sneer on his face, made her temper boil and, she wanted to slap it off his face, so hard, that his teeth would have shattered.

"I've got you, babe. How sweet," Corbat whined and then threatened, "Just make sure you got my fucking money tomorrow night!"

He knows where I am. Bryan knows where I am. I'm sure of it.

She believed it. She had too. She couldn't crack now. She believed in her heart that Bryan was acting on those primal detective instincts of his. He had all those years of experience under his belt. Just the confident tone of his voice signaled something inside of her, he was close. He would rescue her. They would be together again.

She had to make sure, that would happen also. She had to do everything she could, take every precaution, to make her rescue possible. Now that she knew the tracking app on her phone was working, Jessica removed it from her hiding place and tucked it inside her bra. She knew she was going to be moved tonight at ten o'clock.

Morris had told her that earlier, when he brought her a fresh bottle of water, hot cup of coffee, and an egg and sausage sandwich from the local McDonalds. The only thing he didn't know was why she was being moved, where she was being taken, and if it was Bryan, she was being handed over too.

Morris had also given her an old Timex watch that morning, so she could keep track of what time it was.

Nearly two hours had already passed, since he left. All she had time for, was reflection.

Each time Morris had visited her, he opened like a flower waking to the morning sun. He told her about his childhood. He confided in her about the many difficulties he managed to survive through, what his dreams were, and how much he hated being involved in her abduction. He told her, where she was being held, and that it was closed for renovations. Morris vowed he did not know from the beginning, what Corbat had been planning, and she believed him.

Before her left her earlier, Jessica told him where her gun was hidden. She knew in her heart, that the boy's life was in danger. More so, than hers. He was a victim, just like she was. She wanted him to be able to protect himself in case Corbat turned on him. She had told him she was certain it would happen.

Morris knew what kind of man Corbat was. He listened intently, when Jessica had told him, that men like Corbat, wouldn't leave any evidence behind, that tied him to her abduction.

Morris hadn't argued that point. The poor kid was scared out of his wits. And so was she. She just couldn't show how much she was. She had to be strong for the two of them.

She also knew that Corbat had something else up his sleeve, by the snide remarks he had made, after her call with Bryan ended. She just didn't know, what it was.

After Morris left, she fell back into the routine, she had created for herself, so she wouldn't go stir crazy. She cleared more stones as best she could from the area, where she stretched out to sleep. It took her the longest time to do even that, being so constricted with her hands and ankles bound. Her fingertips were sore from digging. Her fingernails were broken. It kept her busy though and helped to pass the time.

She took a break often and attempted to move about. It was difficult, because the surface was uneven and wearing one-inch heels, didn't make it any easier. She lost her balance many times and fell on her hands and knees. The palms of her hands were cut and bleeding. Her pants were torn, and her knees were scraped.

She pushed herself though to keep busy. The small area she managed to clear doubled as a tiny exercise course, where she shuffled slowly, back and forth rather than paced. There was nothing much else she could do to occupy her time. Everywhere she looked, the terrain was impossible to traverse with her ankles cuffed together.

Morris told her she was far away from the attraction areas the visitors toured and where the renovations were taking place. She wondered, if, after she was rescued, whether she'd want to ever come back to this place and take a tour herself.

She chuckled.

"Heck, why not? I always wanted to." She laughed again. "God, now I'm having a conversation with myself."

She shook it off. Just from what she could see of the chamber she was in; it was pretty, magnificent looking.

She learned from Morris, the formations, she looked at constantly were made of limestone. He had pointed out the difference between what was called stalactites and stalagmites. He explained to her, how they were formed, during one of their long talks. She could tell, he loved these caves, and learned everything about them over the years he worked them. Just the excitement and wonder in his voice, wanted her to witness them firsthand, despite being held captive in this place.

She would ask Bryan, to come back with her. She knew that touring the cave, would help her see them in a different light, maybe even help her put this whole nightmare behind her.

Jessica's rumbling stomach woke her from a fitful sleep. When she checked the time on the wristwatch she had been given, it was nearly nine-thirty in the evening. Every inch of her body ached from sleeping on a hard surface so long, that was riddled with jagged stones. The muscles in her arms hurt terribly, as she used them to try and pillow her head. But her constant turning and tossing, as her bindings pulled and raked her skin raw, made it impossible to get comfortable. Her ankles were bleeding now from the cuffs, and she was afraid of an infection setting in. As much as she rinsed them with the water Morris brought frequently, it was hard to keep them constantly clean of dirt.

She was bone tired too. Her eyes were gritty and red from lack of sleep. If it wasn't the sounds of water dripping that kept her awake, it was the bats overhead, the unrecognizable noises of whatever else scurried over the rocks, or her brain, that refused to shut down.

She forced herself into a sitting position and wondered why she hadn't seen Morris by now. He did not stop by to bring her something for lunch, or dinner. Something was terribly wrong. She just knew it.

It wasn't hard to guess that Corbat would be showing up soon and she felt a wave of nausea rise in her chest. This was it. She was either going to walk away from this unscathed, or it may prove her demise. She didn't have to wait long. She could hear someone approaching.

She forced herself to look and confirm it was Corbat and not Morris coming to get her.

"Get up on your feet!" He barked.

She reached out to lean against the large boulder at her side for leverage. Slowly, she managed and wobbled a little, until she righted herself.

Corbat untied the bindings on her hands, and roughly pulled them behind her back and bind them. He squatted down to unlock the cuffs and slipped them in his pocket.

She gazed over her shoulder and asked.

"Where are you taking me? Will Bryan be there?"

He took a rag from his other pocket and forced it into her mouth, clasped a hold of her bindings tightly, and shoved her forward.

"Walk, bitch."

She stumbled often, but this time he did not allow her to fall. He took his time with her. When they entered the elevator, she noticed a washcloth and bottle of water on the floor. He leaned over, uncapped the bottle, and poured the liquid over the washcloth. He rose and his touch was surprisingly tender, as he wiped the dirt from her neck, face, and forehead.

The elevator doors slid open and the bright moonlight shining in through the wide glass doors were blinding and hurt her eyes. She stopped abruptly and leaned over to shield them.

He huffed loudly behind her in exasperation but did not force her forward quite yet. He gave her eyes a moment to adjust, before pushing her forward.

She noticed that the parking lot in front of her was empty. She quickly gazed to the right, and then the left. There wasn't a sign of anyone else in the area. She almost guffawed, from her stupidity.

Bryan wouldn't have parked in the open. He'd be covert somewhere, watching, waiting for the right moment to strike. At least, she silently hoped he was.

The more she looked about, she realized, that they had exited the back of the building. Corbat steered her to the left. There in the distance, was a large u-shaped building. The light that shone from the moon above made it easy for her to decipher this was a motel. She remembered then that Morris had told her lodging was available at the Caverns.

Was there someone waiting in one of those rooms for her? Did he ransom her off to a sex trafficker instead? Was that where Bryan was waiting for her?

Oh, God, no!

Her voice screamed inside her head. She stopped dead, refusing to move. Pushing back against him, and could not help, but whimper.

He punched her square between her shoulder blades, just hard enough to force her forward. His laughter was demonic, and her skin began to prickle with fear.

"Got a surprise for you, princess." He cackled like the Wicked Witch on the Wizard of Oz.

She couldn't stop the tears that began to flow from her eyes. This didn't feel right. Even though he told Bryan to bring his money for her, she knew, that Bryan would have met her the minute she came off that elevator. He would have ended it there.

He stopped her in front of room two-eighteen, turned the doorknob, and pushed her inside. The room was dark and empty. He flipped the switch on the wall to the right, and the room filled with light from a muted bulb.

He kicked the door closed behind him and pushed her forward hard, and she fell face down on the bed.

Something inside her kicked into gear, and she flipped herself around, quicker than she thought she could. She remembered her self-defense trainer had told her it would happen. Her defense mode would flip that switch inside her to protect herself. The moment he got close enough, she mustered every ounce of strength inside of her, and turned her legs into deadly weapons.

Her movements took him totally by surprise, hitting home with striking force.

"You fucking, bitch!" He screamed, as he fell backwards from a well-directed kick to the gut.

Jessica scooted quickly off the bed, balancing herself, ready to strike once more.

Corbat rolled to his side, coughing, and gasping air into his lungs.

His body was sprawled in a way, it blocked her in. She knew, if she moved to the left, he was close enough to reach out and grab her ankle. If she tried shuffling to the right, he could use this thick legs to kick out at her. She waited … waited for him to lift himself up just enough, she'd turn her hip out, side kick out, and have her heel slam him to the side of his head.

The wall clock in the room began to chime the hour, and her head snapped up to note the time … it was ten o'clock,

The door to the room flew open and Jessica's eyes grew wide with horror.

Hal! Dear god, no!

Her eyes would not, could not, revert from his gaze. She watched as his eyes quickly absorbed the situation, reflecting the anger that filled him over what was transpiring in front of him. They scanned over her like an x-ray and his disgust at her appearance was evident.

Without hesitation, without asking what was going on, he slipped his hand inside his breast pocket. He was impeccably dressed in a well-tailored, light grey silk suit. Quickly, he removed a revolver, aimed, and shot Sy Corbat, point blank in the back of his head.

Blood and brain matter splattered on her pant legs and his. She looked down in horror and started to hyperventilate. Her loud moans were muted by the rag still in her mouth. She staggered backward and caught herself.

Hal looked down at the blood stains, and his rage increased. He shot two more bullets into the dead man's body, to vent his anger. Slowly, his gaze traveled the length of her.

Her eyes widened in shocked disbelief.

He shrugged, as though his actions meant nothing, and his tone conveyed his discontent.

"This is not the meeting I had planned for us, sweetheart."

She shot him a look filled with loathing.

He stepped forward, reached for the cloth gagging her mouth, and snapped it out. He held it between his fingers like it was a dirty diaper and let it fall to the floor. He grabbed Corbat's ankles, pulling him off to the side to clear her path.

Jessica reacted immediately, threw herself sideways, rolling across to the other side of the bed. There was plenty of room for her to take a stance. He had to come toward her, and she would take him down, just like she did Corbat.

She looked at the gun in his hand and he sneered. She wasn't stupid. This was a challenge for him. She knew, that as sure as she was standing there, he wouldn't use the gun on her. He wanted her. She was game. He was a hunter. The fun for him, would be disarming her. The look in his eyes told her so. She had to be careful with her words. Her defiance titillated him.

"I won't give up so easily. Not this time, Hal. I'm not the scared, little mouse I was before."

"Ah, yes. I see," he nodded approvingly. "I rather like you this way." He reached down and touched himself, running his palm over the bulge, that she noticed began to grow inside his pants. "See what you do to me, Jessica. Seeing you like this, all defensive, ready to fight for your virtue, gets me hard."

"You are one, sick, bastard, Hal Wilton. If you're really smart, though, you'll just turn around and leave. Bryan knows where I am. The phone I have tucked inside my bra, has a follow me app loaded into it."

There was doubt reflected there in his eyes. She gave him good reason to leave and walk away. He had a lot at stake. If, he got caught, he would lose everything it took him his whole life to build. His reputation would be destroyed. Spending the rest of his life behind bars, would kill him.

A small smile began to grace his lips. She didn't let up.

"Ah. Ah. Ah," she shook her head in warning. "You'd be a fool to doubt me. You've been outsmarted. Leave now, while you've still got time."

There was movement behind him, that caught her attention, and Jessica tried not to react.

Morris quietly stepped over the threshold, stood quietly in the doorway, with a look of hatred marring his features, she never expected to ever see there. His arm was extended, and his hand was holding her gun. It was pointed directly at Hal's back.

She willed him to shoot, before Hal noticed, but, his hesitation proved a deadly one.

She quickly realized; she was standing before an opened area with a double bathroom vanity behind her. She knew Hal saw his reflection in the mirror behind her. She also knew that he saw Morris standing there behind him, a gun pointed at his back.

A slow, evil, grin graced Hal's lips.

Jessica never had the chance to scream out a warning.

Hal spun about and fired.

It was as though everything, that happened, moved in slow motion, as she watched Morris' body fly backwards.

She screamed, like a woman possessed, as she bolted forward, slamming her body into the bastard, with everything she had within her.

It was like some demonic being took control of her body. She wasn't Jessica Wilton anymore; she was someone else.

Hal went down hard. The wind knocked from his lungs.

She flipped over onto her back, pounding the heels of her feet into him with every ounce of strength imaginable. The adrenalin pumping through her veins, gave her the courage and strength she needed to continue.

She was fixated on killing him, as her heels contacted with his throat, his chest, his stomach, the side of his head, leaving ghastly puncture wounds. She could not stop herself. She did not want to. Everything he put her through, the child she lost, her kidnapping, being held prisoner in the cave for days, spurred her on.

She was turned into some one, she did not recognize.

She never saw, or heard Ayden and Bryan enter. Never heard him call out her name. Never felt his arms wrap tightly about her and drag her away from Hal's lifeless body. She never knew, when everything finally went black, and the silence engulfed her completely.

CHAPTER TWENTY-FOUR

Jessica didn't want to open her eyes. The dream was too real. The mattress beneath her was so comfortable and the coverlet tucked around her body, was thick and warm.

Please, she begged silently. *Let me dream for just a little while longer.*

There were consistent noises, starting to penetrate deep into her subconscious, trying desperately to rouse her.

Go away. Please, just go away.

The voice calling to her though was inviting and familiar. It tugged at her heart, made her want to listen.

"Jessica, please, sweetheart … open your eyes. You're safe, honey. Please, just open your eyes."

She heard him.

Or did she, really, her inner voice questioned?

She whimpered in her sleep. She could see his face.

Why can't you find me?

Something warm caressed her cheek, and the touch made her want to open her eyes. Slowly, her eyelids slid open. There was light again. This time, it didn't hurt her eyes. She heard the voice again. She knew it was his. It was Bryan, and his name slipped from her lips in a soft whisper.

"Hey, you, sleepy head."

A smile caressed her lips, when her eyes focused, and those gorgeous blue orbs of his greeted her.

He leaned in close, touched his lips to hers, to let her know it was no longer a dream, but something beautifully real.

She was fully awake now and aware that others were in the room. She looked about and a puzzled look was on her face.

Her Aunt stepped forward, and clasped Jessica's hand tenderly in her own.

"Hello, sweet girl."

Jessica smiled softly.

"You're in a private room, dear, at Cobleskill Regional Hospital. When the doctor tells us you're strong enough to travel, we'll fly you home."

Her voice was weak, but audible as she replied, "I'm strong enough."

Soft laughter filled the air, and her Aunt's broad smile, made her smile again too.

"Want to sit up, dear?"

Jessica nodded and Bryan assisted her.

She gazed at him lovingly and a gush of emotion escaped her.

"You saved me."

He sat upon the edge of her bed and drew her into his arms. She couldn't stop the tears that slipped from her eyes, or the sobs shaking her shoulders. She was overwhelmed with relief, and sadness that Morris had died, trying to save her too. She clung to Bryan desperately, wanting to make sure this truly wasn't a dream, that she was free of the cave, free of her tormentor, and free from Hal.

It felt splendorous to feel the strength of his arms about her, to smell the scent of his cologne fill her nostrils, the warmth of his cheek against her, and his lips, those beautiful, exquisite lips, grazing her skin. It was over. It was over. The nightmare and horror were over.

The whizz of a motor and wheels crossing the tile floor of her hospital room caught her attention, and Jessica opened her eyes.

"Morris!" She bellowed happily. "Morris, you're alive!"

"I sure is, mam. Happy to be too."

She released Bryan, and outstretched her arms, her fingers waving invitingly for him to move closer.

Morris obliged, and Bryan moved off the bed, so he could get closer. He lifted his hands, and Jessica clasped onto them, as if for dear life.

Her voice still cracked with emotion.

"I can't tell you, how happy … I am to see … that you survived."

Her eyes darted to Bryan's and pleaded.

"He's not to blame. He can't be arrested. Morris was bullied, and beaten, and threatened by Corbat, Bryan. He –"

"Breathe, Jessica, breathe. We know, honey. Morris told us everything. We just were waiting for you to confirm, and you just did. We believe you, and we'll make sure he's not prosecuted."

He directed his attention to a man in the room and she recognized him.

"You're … you're Bryan's friend, the detective."

The man nodded and stepped forward.

"Yes, mam, Det. Ayden Tyler. Mr. Levitt won't be arrested. I promise you that."

"You helped Bryan, didn't you … to find me."

Bryan interjected. "I couldn't have done it without him either."

She reached out her hand, and the Detective moved swiftly to accept it.

"Thank you. From the bottom of my heart."

And then, it was like a movie began to play out in her mind.

Her hands flew to her mouth, and she moaned painfully, as her eyes glazed with horror.

"No! No!" she screamed, as tears streamed from her eyes, and she shook her head wildly. "My, god. Dear, god, Bryan," she gasped loudly. "I … I … killed him. I killed, Hal."

Bryan ran to her side and pulled her into his embrace.

She clung to him desperately, her body convulsing from the heart, piercing sobs wracking her body.

"No, baby, no. You didn't." He rocked her tenderly. "He didn't die, Jessica. You didn't kill that bastard."

Slowly, she pulled back from his embrace. She looked deeply into his eyes.

He nodded, smiling softly. "He's where he deserves to be … behind bars."

Tears still streamed from her disbelieving eyes, and she looked up at Ayden for confirmation.

Ayden nodded too and added.

"He'll be spending the rest of his life in a six by eight-foot cell." He directed his attention to Bryan and winked. "I've got a lot of paperwork to fill out, because of you," he replied jokingly. "Once you're on your feet, mam, and ready to sit down with me, I'll need a deposition from you about everything that happened, so we can close this case." He looked at everyone in the room, nodded respectively and exited.

She sighed deeply, content in knowing, that all would be well again.

Bryan directed his attention to both Morris and her Aunt.

"If you two don't mind, I'd like to spend some alone time with my girl."

Florence walked over to Morris and laid her arm across his shoulder. "Come, dear. Let's go back to your room for a short while, and we can discuss your future."

The moment they exited; Bryan closed the door to her room for more privacy and returned to sit on the edge of her bed.

"I'm sorry your association with me, pulled you into one horrifying situation. Can you ever forgive me?"

"Forgive you. You can't blame yourself for what happened. This was all, because of Hal. He concocted this whole scheme. I certainly don't blame you. I … I just want to get back to normal."

He chuckled lightly. "You call, what we do, normal?"

"Well," she shrugged, "maybe, what I really mean is, you and me."

"I like that answer, even better."

She reached for his hands, drew them to her lips, and kissed them tenderly. She couldn't stop the tears that misted her eyes. She knew she wasn't going to cry … outright sob anyway. She was just overwhelmed by the emotion she felt for this man.

"When I was alone, in that cave, I couldn't stop thinking of you. The thought of my time spent with you played over and over in my mind. Those thoughts of you kept me going and gave me strength, and made me smile, and want to get through it all. It also made me realize, how much I love you and want to spend the rest of my life with you."

His eyes misted like a beautiful, blue ocean, and she knew in her heart, he felt the same. She wanted to hear the words ... words she had never heard spoken before. At that very moment, she needed all he could give. And he did not disappoint her, or keep her waiting long.

"I want to feel the breath from your lips caress my skin forever. I want to lie with you in my arms at night, in a home we create as our own. I want to be the father of our children, your lover, your husband, and the only closest friend you'll ever need."

Her breath hitched in her throat at his words and she gasped, as he pulled a tiny, velvet box from his pants pocket.

He opened the lid, and she saw the embossed name 'Neal Lane' at first and then the most gorgeous Emerald-cut yellow diamond. She didn't give him time to ask the question. The look in his eyes spoke volumes. She threw her arms tightly about his neck and lathered his face with sweet kisses as she lyrically spoke, "Yes. Yes. Yes. A thousand times yes."

The End

I hope you enjoyed reading 'A Pawn for Malice'. If you would, please write a review on the site where you purchased it, I would truly appreciate it. Not only do I so enjoy reading your comments, it helps promote more sales, and for others to discover my book as well. You'll note from the genres listed below, I'm a pretty diverse author and pen all my titles under the same name.

I'm always hosting special promotions and giveaways, so please feel free to follow me on any of my social media platforms I've noted below to stay connected and keep abreast of what's new and upcoming. Thank you so very much for purchasing 'A Pawn for Malice' and becoming a part of my romance family.

My Other Books

Historical Romance ~ Iroquois Series
Wind Warrior ~ Book 1
Captive Heart ~ Book 2
Captive Warrior ~ Book 3

Contemporary
This Too Shall Pass

Suspense Thriller
Keeper's Watch ~ The Wind

Contemporary – Love Song Standards Series
Unchained Melody
Strangers In The Night
For Once In My Life
Can't Help Falling In Love
At Last
Chances Are

Upcoming Titles
All The Way
It's Impossible
Sincerely
Unforgettable

I would so very much love to connect with you and hope you'll follow me on any one of my Social Media Networks

https://www.facebook.com/Cynthia.Roberts.Author

https://www.pinterest.com/RomanceCynthia/

https://instagram.com/romanceauthorcynthiaroberts/

https://www.goodreads.com/author/show/3433035.Cynthia_Roberts

https://www.romanceauthorcynthiaroberts.com

cynthia@romanceauthorcynthiaroberts.com